# THE MEMORIALIST

# THE
# MEMORIALIST

*A Novella and Stories*

# Marshall Terry

Three Forks Press
Dallas

**THREE FORKS PRESS**
**P.O. BOX 823461**
**DALLAS, TEXAS 75382**

ISBN 1-893451-10-0

Printed in the United States of America

First Edition

To My Family

# THE MEMORIALIST

Vol. 4 of "Northway"

The "Northway" Chronicle:

# THE MEMORIALIST

## 1.

I am embarrassed to say that I felt that my only brother passed away at an inopportune time, for me, and I am sure, also for him. It was just like Luke to blunder into a room, into a situation, into death.

It was that I was just then already tired of death. Had by then spoken at too many memorial services, was even myself thinking of myself as "the Memorialist." I thought of writing a story with that title but couldn't form it, resolve it. Instead, that Fall before Luke's death, I had made a list of those in my university—friends, colleagues and the former student—who had "passed away."

Those Who Died This Term: The wife of a good friend, herself a friend, we three had hiked from the college on the High where we were teaching that summer across the fields and to the stream to the Trout together. My colleague and so close friend as to be a brother, Max, who had come in smiling at me towering over my desk saying, "They tell me I have these little thing-ies in my head," and soon passed on, taking half the poker times and quaffing times and softball times I'd ever known with him. Miss Phoebe Hoagland, age 96, whole Women's Movement of her time, bright and lovely, pioneer woman in our English department who'd brought Phi Beta Kappa to this campus and when I'd come here as a student taught me. Looking at the library and the letters she had left I had found correspondence from the early 1920s, before she had gone up and by God, sir, taken her Ph.D. at a leading university and turned her dissertation into a book and been first of her sex to become full professor and be chairperson of the department. Among the correspondence I found scrawled letters from a jovial young man from her hometown in love with Miss Phoebe. But the young man could not spell. That must have been it. She could not have married a man who could not spell the most familiar words! And so the die was cast, her passion turned to ideas, travel, books.

This is but a partial list of those who died that term.

Max I had loved. I still have trouble realizing his great presence is gone. He had been exactly my age and is gone.

Maybe it—the unresolvability of it—was that I did not do a memorial for Max.

Then I had sat in the circle of my fellow writer-teachers in and around the university, some of them my former students, and said a sentence or two for the prize-winning poet on our faculty who had died, passing away on his couch, like a small shaggy bear, obese and brilliant. I remembered the poet as a boy, a student just beginning poetry, giving a first formal reading to us of his words, stammering, flushed, round and vulnerable in a bright green suit.

Enough? No more additions to the list? Not quite. Not quite. One more. Dan. At thirty-two, dear God! Humorous, quick—publishing more and more, cascading postcards with gnomic loving messages to me, his teacher—Eaten up by the damnable pernicious thing in less than a year!

I had introduced a reading at a downtown club in Dan's honor, said a few words about him. That was as close as I could get to that.

These were my students, not my "brothers." They did not include my half-brother Jake, whose father had married my mother their second time around, who'd shot himself. Or my rebellious, lost brother-in-law Orlando, who by then not able to talk through his voice box, mouthed angrily at me, wild-eyed, before he slipped back away to coma.

And then, out of the blue, unexpected and inappropriate, my brother. My own very real damn brother.

Lord forgive me. What a way to put it! The most loving, loyal brother a brother ever had.

I found a file and in it a stack of letters through the many years, from childhood on. Wry, ironic, witty, shielded, full of what my brother Luke had said of himself, his "reverse inferiority-superiority complex." Dear God, Luke could write. Why had he never written anything? Had he? Was it hidden away somewhere? Would Luke's daughter find the Great American, the Great Academic, the great Neo-Rabelaisian or Dickensian novel in a drawer or filing cabinet?

What made it more raw for me than the loss even, when his great weight slumped over on his bed from his wheelchair and died, was that we were so out of touch. That in all these years, these forty years, telling myself from time to time I should, I had never gone up there to see him, to see Luke's place where he lived and taught his whole career. That there was no final word, no last embrace. That he was gone.

Luke had retired. He had moved up above the town, off the beaten paths of his friends. He had lain dead a week before someone thought to check on him.

It was that finally my beaming, spirited little brother—which was how he suddenly came back to me—who had grown into the large curmudgeon had been so damnably alone.

When they had cut off his foot from the diabetes Luke had taken to the wheelchair at home, worn the prosthetic foot when going out. "Goddamn thing cost five thousand dollars!" he'd chortled to me over the phone. Irony: His feet were big. One of his nicknames, from our father, growing up, had been "Feet." Luke had several nicknames from his father, all pejorative, "Feet" and "Fong" and "Fatso"—"Frog."

Our salesman/merchandising father hadn't understood this burr-headed boy, a round ball on stalk legs, who read Havelock Ellis at twelve and liked classical music and opera and strange films, not baseball, football and TV. Our father had been amazed when both of his very different sons had become, of all things, English professors!

I must say, Luke was the one with the Ph.D., the deep and constant reading and study of Elizabethan and Victorian English literature, the single devotion to the teaching of his first-generation college students, the utter scorn of the idiot administrators who through the years were turning his liberal arts college into a "comprehensive" university with more and more business and vocational programs attached. Luke's occasional letters and our rare phone conversations were full of his reaction to this idiocy.

Lately he had stopped responding to my e-mail messages. It took him a while to wheel to the phone. He grunted that if you rang twelve times he might decide to answer; but he rarely did.

We had not spoken for months.

Through the time between the news of Luke's death and the memorial service on his campus at which they asked me to speak I stopped being shocked and began to fill up with guilt and sorrow, until I came to dread going up for the service.

But of course I had to go. Finally and too late, I would go.


Gloria and I flew up, changing to the smaller plane to Newburgh in the Cincinnati airport. It was not really Cincinnati, where Luke and our younger sister Joy and I grew up, but miles across the river in northern Kentucky. Gloria did not like the idea of flying in the smaller plane. "Why don't you call Mary Stewart?" she said as we waited. Rob Stewart had been in my class in our school on Indian Hill, in the class of twelve. He'd been the slow halfback on the football team. I was a guard and opened holes for Rob to run through, but not often. He and Mary had "gone steady" from the eighth grade through high school and college, then married. He had been one of my oldest friends, that is, most longtime. Rob had not changed a jot or a tittle through the years, except for becoming more conservative, if possible, a devotee of the N.R.A. He had died of heart failure several years ago. "Not this time," I said. "Maybe when we come back through."

You went through a part of life with a person, I reflected, then did not keep in touch, then he was gone. Sometimes I fought against this terrible obligation to give to each life its identity, its specialness, its due. Where did it come from? Was it some mid-twentieth century American caveat we'd had ingrained in us—the individual, the worth of each human being, each human life is a story to be told—ingrained by our fathers, mother, teachers? Had it been America's deep need to pose the worth of any one American against the totalitarianism of the worldwide menace of Communism? Anyway, Rob Stewart was a steady, sweet boy, I would have had to say of him if I had been called to be his memorialist. Who out of fear of all the forces that were going to come and attack him and take his inheritance had given thousands to the N.R.A. and filled his house on a hill and then the house in Florida with their plaques, and guns.

"When do you think Luke began to change?" Gloria said. She had been kind to him when Luke had come, flunked out, floundering, down here to enroll in my place, and made it finally to a degree, and then went with Sally and their child on down to Austin for the Ph.D.

"When Sally left him, and he got—oh, not just overweight and drinking and smoking—but really sick. Had to retire, for the medical benefits. It was the last thing he wanted."

"I thought he had given up the smoking and the drinking."

"I hope so. He would have had to, with the diabetes. Except, on one of the last times we talked, I heard ice clinking in the glass, and asked if he was drinking. 'Oh, I have one now and then,' he said."

Gloria rolled her eyes, as so often through the years she'd done at Luke.

As our small jet stuttered its way to Newburgh, where we would meet our daughter and then drive on to Luke's college over in Pennsylvania, I tried to think of what I would say, to that community, Luke's own place, of Luke. I thought I should say something formal, serious; and took pen and pad and began to sketch it out. . . .    It must elevate Luke, elevate my own thoughts about him, bring significance to the occasion. . . .

(Oh boy, here I went again. Yes, yes, as brother Luke would say, in the voice he did of who was it? Larson P. Whipsnade?)

*I am comforted* (I was) *in my brother's death by the knowledge that he helped to wake to learning generations of the students he loved to teach.* ("Damn right, Bruth'! I did that, all right. I taught the little bastards well!")

*Luke was a sweet and loyal person.* ("Sweet? Dear God, Sir! You have just above called that cornball Rob Stewart 'sweet' and now you are calling me of all the sentimental preposterousnesses your mind is capable of, sweet?") (Yes, you were, as a boy and, I think, really always. Oh, almost unbearable: the note Luke sent me when I, big brother Mark, was about to graduate from high school and go off to college and we would be separated for the first time. Luke wrote that we would always be the Corsican brothers, if one was hurt the other felt the blow. . . .)

*With a sharp edge for truth, teaching always towards freedom and directness of thought and away from hypocrisy and cant. . .*

And: *Growing up in our semi-rural Ohio, my brother believed in the good earth and in good sense.* . . .    Yes.

*His reading was deep: in his mind were*—Be careful, Orator. Well, it was true, his mind was the place he mainly dwelled. *In his mind were many mansions, including those of irony and humor.*

And: *Like mine, his career was spent in one good place.*

And I was his older brother and, withal, loved him, and might I suppose be excused this present devastating feeling of being left—save for sister Joy—with the only memory of our growing up, the mythology of the family, the romance and tragedies of our parents, the love of grandparents, the sense of those acres our father brought us to and worked so hard to cultivate.

*And am, his brother, also professor in your discipline though I do not know you, pleased to join you in commemorating his service and devotion to your community of learning.*

Very good, Sir. Most excellent good. Well said, oh well said! Take a bow, and try not make wind as you leave the stage.

We drove over to Pennsylvania from the Hudson valley with our daughter Glory and her teenage daughter Terri. We drove through the town and found the campus and, among the old stone buildings, the Victorian house where Luke had officed so many years. We joined my sister Joy and her husband Jim, who had driven up from Texas in their new Explorer, and Luke's former wife Sally and her new husband Felix and met Luke's friends and colleagues there: the new chair of the department, who had been Luke's disciple yet was going into administration anyway: the "mad Irish" fellow Luke had fished and drunk with; other members of the department; some former students. I had met some of the colleagues at the MLA meetings in New York years ago. The president of the university and his wife and the provost were in attendance at the outdoor service. Several of Luke's colleagues spoke. A female colleague quoted Shelley and quoted Luke. The young new chair and the "Mad Irishman" spoke. It was clear to me that they had loved Luke.

When it came my turn I did not give voice to the words I had written out but spoke briefly. Like Mr. Pickwick, I said, my brother had been that rare thing, "a good man." My brother and I had spoken often of this place and Luke's commitment to it. I felt Luke's spirit with us. Luke would love this tree.

Luke's daughter had brought in a graceful young tree to be planted outside the window to Luke's office. It came to light that Luke had been devoted to the environment, more so than I had known. The tree bole was wrapped in burlap, and after the words many gathered on the green grass under blue sky of the fine spring day took up shovel and mock-helped to plant the tree. When handed the shovel I didn't get much soil but just flipped a bit of fertilizer into the hole. I could hear old Luke laughing at me. I knew that Luke's bulk had been cremated; I did not know what they had done with the ashes.

After this brief ceremony the provost, as provosts will, confessed to me that he was still actively engaged in scholarly research. The president, in a dark blue jacket with their logo on the pocket, and his pleasant wife strolled over to where I stood, a little shakily, with Luke's "Irish" buddy and smiled and said to me, "We had our disagreements, but I respected him and I believe your brother really did like me." "He hated you," said the "mad Irishman" as the pair strolled away.

"I suppose you have been a bloody rebel—intransigent, scorning the bastards—at your place, too?" Billy said.

"Why no," I said. "I helped with the philosophy, was always in the planning. The presidents, all along the way, were my friends."

"Oh—Sure. You were chairman, there, when you were just a boy, weren't you? Luke was proud of that. He went around those days telling that his brother was the bloody chairman of the department and would be glad to give us all jobs down there!" He laughed.

At the reception afterwards at the house of a bluff fellow who claimed Northway kin with us Luke's daughter gave me the old railroad watch her father had carried. It was thoughtful. Everyone drank beer and wine, inside and outside the house, and talked literature and Luke. Our effervescent sister Joy was the hit of the party. She was outgoing, a bit outrageous, laughing, cheerful, loud. Everyone said she reminded them of Luke in his sociable moods, and she grooved on it. When Gloria and Glory and Terri and I were going out the door, leaving to drive back east, I had my first word with Luke's older grandson, a funny kid who looked like Luke when he was a boy. Luke in these last years had adored his grandsons. They had been, I believe, his link to vitality in his narrowing life. "Grandpa taught me to do this," the boy said, crossing and popping out his eyes and pulling his mouth down like a clown.

A young fellow in the department, standing by the wall inside the house drinking mugs of beer, had said he regularly went out to "do shots" with Luke, even just recently. A little ginger-haired adjunct woman in a cowboy vest and boots allowed that old Luke was her drinking buddy, they'd do boilermakers and eat hot wings together often, up until he dropped dead.

So Luke was happy. Or anyway had friends, was not as lonely as I had thought.

"Last spring," said the host, a large man in cavernous pants upheld by braces, "he'd lost his foot, so he'd sit out in his back yard, and he impressed several of us to get his garden dug, and then he would sit there and instruct us just how to plant the garden like he'd done it—the so and so's just in half an inch, the beans exactly this deep and the rows just so far apart and—so on—just how we should put in the tomato plants. And get furious, give us holy hell, if we didn't do it exactly right! Hell, Mark, look around here—I don't have the time or energy to plant a garden or take care of my own place, and I'm spending hours doing his!"

"He could be a tyrant," said the new young chairman, his disciple.

My sister Joy waved happily at us as we left. She and Jim were going to stay a few days with Luke's daughter, then drive slowly back in the Explorer—she could put the seat on her passenger side down and lie back peacefully as Jim drove—visiting his sister in Tennessee along the way.

Back here on my campus I walked the halls and sat thankfully in my office overlooking the paths and spires and looked beyond to the outline of the tall buildings of the city. I greeted colleagues so enthusiastically they thought I had gone daft, grateful for this gift of life, the ability to greet them; driven to think, now in one moment and then another, of my other "brothers," now gone, once so close. I stopped in daily to visit with Si, several years past retirement, who was working on a new book, vigorous and alert. "How'd it go?" he asked.

"A little strange. Glad I went."

The younger members of my department, gay and black and Indian, went by. My old friend Dale went by rubbing at his great white ruff of beard. He poked his head in to greet Roscoe, our curmudgeon, who informed me of several current follies in the department and on campus of which he kept close track. The British flag hung on his office door and he would be off to the land it represented at term's end. My old pals, the other writers, poet and novelist, nodded to me as we all staggered up and down the stairway from our offices to classes to meetings and back to the endless conferences that close attention to student writing necessitate.

A little later that spring the historian and novelist T. Jimmy Wyatt who lived down in the center of the state died at a fairly advanced age. I and several other members of the fellowship of the Institute of Letters traveled from wherever we were to the graveside service for T. Jimmy. We stood outside the tent for family with the grave yawning nearby under warm sun on a sultry day listening to the burly minister speak, and to a big bird in a tree that stridently began to compete with him. Old John, cross-eyed, bow-legged, a little humped in the shoulders now from honest work farming and writing, our philosopher-sage, leaned to my ear as we stood there and said, "Mockingbird's singing for T. Jimmy."

## 2.

My sister Joy was happy that day. I was glad to see her happy, enjoying the occasion. Her loyalty had always been intense. This day I was moderating a lighthearted faculty panel at the Homecoming luncheon of some of us teachers who had been around here and at it for a long time. Joy was, like me and as Luke had been, an alum, and a lot of the brass of the university and the big gun alumni were present, and I and the other faculty were that blend of significant and funny that you want to be on such occasions, and there was good applause—even from Herb the young president for I ended it to the minute on time which was what counted with him—and then Joy was strutting, proud, around the room and to me, and we had our picture taken together by the university photographer.

Everyone said that Joy and I had the "Northway look," that ruddy complexion and near-Chinese eye-set and that we had almost the same profile, the sharp nose, squashed on the face of our brother Luke, and the Northway lip, so often curled in laughter.

I was glad that she was here and happy, energized so that the strange numbness in her legs and feet was overridden, smiling, bluff, loud as always in her speech and laughter, her girth draped in one of her long loose dresses.

She wobbled up to me as I hung out in the crowd before the event, grabbing my arm for balance. "What do you know, wise and wonderful brother mine?" she said.

"You need to see a real doctor, an orthopedist," I said.

"Oh, I don't know," she said. She seemed scared to find out what was really wrong. She'd had enough "stuff" as our mother would have said, already.

Afterward, eyes shining, the event a success, her brother a star on this minor stage, she waited with her quiet husband to have their picture taken as I greeted former students who came to the dais to remind me who they were and what decade of the four they'd been in my first-year composition or my creative writing or my literature classes.

Following the luncheon and its aftermath, with a wave to her and Jim, I walked across the campus to my office in my classic columned building and sat at my desk and looked out my window down the stretch of crossing walks and Georgian buildings and on to the tops of the tall buildings of the city, and took the carved flowing head and back of a feathered Indian that our mother's sister's husband had fashioned from driftwood from a California beach and which Joy and I exchanged at our birthday lunch each year and set it back beside me on my desk. The young people who came in for conferences liked the curving torso of the Indian, its high feathers, its sense of fluidity and hope and vitality coming up out of its driftwood base; took it perhaps as they did so many things as a symbol, and in a personal sense it was. It stood for so much lost that only Joy and I remembered.

Later, when I had the news of Joy and the tears lay too deep for words and I came into this office looking out to the campus symmetry and must think of what to say of her, I took the feathered brave, the fragile carving, and put it on top of the cabinet behind me, only sensing and not seeing it there.

Each year we had our lunch together between December and February. Between Scorpio and Aquarius, between our birthdays. The one who had it would bring the Indian and we would exchange it formally. We would always laugh that Uncle Scott himself—dark. handsome. piercing-eyed—had looked like the Indian he'd carved, or anyway like an Indian. Our father Mark Northway had called his brother-in-law "Chief Rain-in-the-Face." That did not mean he was dour, did not mean much of anything, anymore than such assignments and labels meant anything more than convenient tags for white middle class families in America in the Twenties, Thirties, Forties. Our father liked to label everyone around him, Luke as "Feet," Joy his darling "little sunbeam." (Was ordained to be so, and so was.) I was "Bo" all the way up, originating in something having to do with my looking like "a little Bohunk" that passed between my grandfathers when they first beheld me in my incubator in the hospital shortly after my rather early birth.

Since Joy did not make it to that mid-birthday time that year I was left to conjure up and reflect on our lunch meeting of the year before.

Smiling at first, she passed the Indian over to me. But her bright dress and scarf belied the language of her stout body. She had wavered as she walked. Her eyes sat in tight pouches. Her hair wisped on her head. There was a sense of pain about her, and the smile was a thin crack in the pain. By coffee after the Greek food we could talk a little about the problems that troubled her.

In their thirties, her sons were boys no longer, though they seemed to be. She had mothered them, protected them, close as any mother lion. They had brought her happiness, puzzlement, now grief. It was the old odd case: they adopted the one, thinking they could not have children, then the other was quickly born. They were the same age. The adopted boy was physically different from them, and was different from them; goodhearted but just not in tune with them. The natural son was a star athlete, deep in their mold, moody but loving. Now I could tell that the one boy had hurt her, and the other was getting close to it.

"He was searching for his birth mother, and he found her," Joy said. "Tried to call his father, but he didn't want to talk to him."

The boy she had always fully thought of as a son had for the time rejected her.

The last time I had seen this boy alarmed me. He came to my office. He was not employed and was thinking of going back to college for another degree. He had an edge to him. I wondered if he was not sleeping in his car. I called Joy and Jim to tell them of my worry. "Maybe he is," said Jim, weighed by the years of propping up the boy, sending him out and taking him back in.

I never knew just what the boy said or did that wounded her.

"And," I said the other boy's name. "How is he?"

The anger, truculence that had reddened her face went out as if leached, her cheeks turned white with sadness. The natural son had now separated from his wife and the child Joy adored. The son had grim moods and had gone into a silence, a cave away from all of them. Then disappeared. They had not heard from him in months. Now as I reflect on this it has been a year, and we do not know where he is or whether he is alive or dead.

After coffee I walked her down to the parking lot below—she almost could not make it down the angled concrete slope—and lectured her on seeing about this numbness in her legs and helped her lift herself into the vehicle, that Explorer she loved so much.

As it happened, she had an appointment with the orthopedist, finally, for the Monday after the Saturday in December, and the day before her birthday, when she was killed.

It was a rainy Saturday just before noon. Gloria and I came in from a run to the store. The phone rang. I picked it off the kitchen wall, just repainted whitest white. A woman's voice asked for and greeted me.

"This is Mary Hagedorn, chaplain at the Baylor Hospital in Ennis, Texas, Mark."

A chaplain, calling me by my first name. That dull thud, that click that comes as the door opens in your mind.

"Yes."

"About James Linsley. He is with us here. I believe he is your brother-in-law."

"How is he? I mean, what—"

"Oh, he's all right. He's in the I.C. unit, but—not serious. I have talked to him. He wanted me to call you."

"My sister—Mrs. Linsley. Joy. She's my sister."

"Yes, sir."

"How is she?"

"I'm afraid—She didn't make it, Mark."

"I see."

"James is very bruised—upset. He was driving. They hydroplaned—I believe—in the rain and crossed the median and hit an oncoming tractor-trailer."

"Please tell him—"

"Would you like to speak to him? I can transfer you to him."

"Oh. Yes—"

"I'm so sorry. I wish you God's peace." She did it well.

"What is it?" Gloria said.

"It's Joy."

Gloria questioned, but I shook my head as Jim came on the line. He sounded like a boy worn out from running.

"I'm so sorry, Mark," he said.

"We lost your sister," he said.

"I couldn't help it," he said.

"No."

"I tried to steer but we went off the road and it was so—I couldn't steer it."

Then he said, "It was instantaneous."

He said that he had talked to Sarah, Joy's close friend here in town and she and her daughter were already on the way to pick him up and bring him home. He said that the Explorer was totaled. That was all he ever said about it. I said that we would see him the next day.

Later the friend, Sarah, said she had seen the Explorer. It was twisted into a U shape. She said that Joy, as she liked to do traveling in this vehicle, was lying down sleeping when they "hydroplaned" across the lake of water on the highway across the median of the interstate into the oncoming eighteen-wheeler. Jim only said, when we went to see him, and the times after that, that he missed her, and how he was coming along in healing his broken ribs and toes and bruises. He contained all his grief and pain and shock within. He did not want to tell the story of Joy's death. He said they'd had a good, relaxing time on their trip down for a few days to the coast. She had told me she was looking forward to it, was taking puzzles, books.

I would have liked to know what book she was reading; what puzzle she was working.

Jim's sisters came and cleared Joy's clothes from her house. We went there to visit with them. Jim's sisters and he talked of their parents, the houses they had grown up living in, their past and present differences. They looked at a cache of old photographs Joy had. Luke's daughter, who had come for the service as we had gone to her father's, and the sisters could not tell who some of the people in the photographs were. They were our grandparents and aunts and uncles, Uncle Pete and Aunt Prudence, and so on. I drank wine and visited with the sisters and their husbands, one of them like Jim my former student. "Did you ever have your sister in class?" Henry said.

"Not really. By chance as a first-year she showed up in one of my sections. And every time that hour I said anything, profound or foolish, introducing the course, or looked out the window searching for my thoughts, Joy went into fits and gales of laughter! Right after class I transferred her into someone else's section."

It made us all laugh, a little.

I kept it short as I spoke for the family at Joy's service. Joy's spirit or maybe it was sunshine (I believe that it was both) flooded the church. People filled it. Until I wrote the obituary for the paper and then beheld all the people that Joy knew and worked with—some came from other towns and cities to honor her—all her friends and colleagues in the years of community service and volunteer work—I had not really comprehended her life.

I recalled her as a girl growing up on our Indian Hill, watering the tomatoes and feeding the chickens as her brothers hoed weeds, all of us doing the tasks our father assigned us, Joy adoring her father, being apprentice to her mother. I was now the only one who remembered her as that happy girl.

The former pastor and the present pastor spoke truly of Joy, for they had known her. But it was the son, the adopted son, who brought the resolution she would have loved.

He went down to the pulpit and faced us and said, "It has been a privilege for me to be a member of this family."

Then the pianist beat out "Amazing Grace," and the boy, the erstwhile Prodigal, stood in line with us as we received.

Where was the other son, the present Prodigal?

Jim said, well, he knows where he is. Sooner or later he'd come home. He'd be surprised.

## 3.

A couple of months later I came into my house in the late afternoon and collected the mail (comprising one letter and many opportunities to support worthy causes) and noticed that the newly painted wall by the front door had already cracked, a wavy line going from the corner of the ceiling almost down to the wooden frame. We could have the painter come back and smooth it out and paint again so it wouldn't show. Then a month later the crack would come again. This old house was not built on sand but on a dry creek bed that shifted back and forth, as we had known when we moved in thirty years ago. I'd had some colleagues in the engineering school come and take a look at the foundation. They said they thought it would last as long as we did.

I read the lone letter before I checked the messages on the answering machine. It was from an old friend now retired and living outside the city expressing sympathy for the recent sudden death of my sister. She offered condolences in the form of parallel tragedies and mishaps in her sphere. Her best friend had called on the new century's eve to tell her she had breast cancer. Her friend down the way called to tell her he was having a heart attack. (She could hear the ambulance coming in the distance.) Another friend's daughter had gone to the funeral of one of her students who had been murdered in Ponca City, Oklahoma, and fell down the church steps flat on her face and broke her nose and split her lip. "And now," our friend wrote, "I receive your letter informing me that your sister was killed in an automobile accident before Christmas, how tragic."

I almost smiled as I put the letter down and punched the button on the answering machine.

The wavering voice came on addressing me with all the force of my Midwestern roots, the voice of my Uncle Pete, favorite brother-in-law of my father. "Bo, or I suppose I should say, Mark. . . . This is your Uncle Pete in Cedar Rapids, Iowa. Prudence McDear, your aunt —" He said, "ahnt." "—passed away this afternoon peacefully at about three-twenty-seven. She was, you know, eighty-five. We are having a service. Give me a jingle."

I heard it with a stirring of guilt where my heart had already drooped from the grief connected with Luke and Joy. I had meant, meant for years, to go and see them up in Iowa where they had lived so long, wonderful, wacky Prudence and my boyhood hero Uncle Pete. Called her "Aunty Pru," so warm-hearted; she'd been my babysitter there in Cleveland when I was a baby and she was in high school. The last time I had tried to talk to her long distance she seemed puzzled, had said in the midst of it to someone apparently nearby, "My family are calling me. What do you think they want?"

I decided to go up for the funeral or memorial service, whatever it might be. Gloria said she thought I should.

Uncle Pete sounded surprised and pleased when I called back to tell him I was coming. He would get me a reservation at the Old Mill Run motel not too far from his condo. It was cheap but clean. Greg was there, his son, he'd driven from Michigan. He would have him call me. Greg's family was on the way. His other son, Pete Jr., was going to come over from Nebraska with his bunch. Anything else? "Okay, Bo, I'll hang up now. This must be costing you an arm and a leg."

As my uncle hung up, I—"Bo"—almost thought it was my father's voice saying that. My father had—on his own, deploring FDR, whom I now admired from an historical perspective—made it through the Great Depression and lived every day of his life after that with the sure knowledge that it would come again. Uncle Pete, my father's younger disciple, followed the same basic philosophy.

And I myself, the character who used to be, growing up, "Bo," could I be, really now, approaching my own three-score and-ten? I heard my Aunty Pru's wacky laugh from back in time, as if this was a wonderful joke on both of us.

I talked to my cousin Alma, daughter of my mother's and Prudence's other sister, who had preceded them in death. It would be hard for Alma to come. I negotiated for myself a "bereavement fare" with the airline—a gentleman in his late sixties traveling to the funeral of his aged aunt!

Uncle Pete's son Greg called. He was a minister with not only a fundamentalist flock but also a flock of his own. He was the second son and so the one closest to his father. I couldn't remember just how many kids Greg had, had never met them. I'd seen Greg several years ago when he'd come into town for a conference of Christian Athletes and stayed with Joy. He'd been a Minnesota Viking, a college star, and a big good-hearted kid. The other boy (fifty-year-old boys these were) had a company, did some sort of outdoor work in Nebraska. He had about as many children as his brother. Concentrating, pulling the threads together, remembering Prudence's holiday notes and cards, I thought that Greg and Edie had seven, Pete Jr. and his wife had five. I could not have named them if Salvation depended on it.

Though we hardly knew each other Greg and I talked easily. He was glad to connect again. He told me of the disruption, sadness and tension of Prudence's decline and his father's putting her in Golden Oaks.

"The service is on Monday," he said. "I'm glad you're coming. I'll meet you at the airport. Pete—my dad—has moved into a condo. It's a Christian condominium. It's across town from where we always lived. She's going to be cremated. We're having a little problem, difference of opinion. I want my kids to see grandma, to see her laid out in the coffin. Have a family viewing. Some of them haven't seen her for a year or more. He says why go to all the trouble and expense of embalming her, fixing her up, just for the family, and then cremating. He has a point, but I think it would be good for the kids, for all of us, to see her all fixed up, to have a good final memory together.

"He's worried about the cost, of course. He's worried about his money, anyway. He's not wealthy, and he may last a while. He's got the palsy, and he was in that wreck, but if he can get his equilibrium back. . . I told him it wouldn't amount to any more than having her in Golden Oaks another month or so.

"I'll tell you, Bo. We went by the funeral home, and he liked the young guy who owns it, he's the son of the old owner Dad knew. 'Say,' he says to him, 'what's a coffin going for these days?' He was shocked. So I don't know."

Gloria took me to the airport. I had my heavy coat over my arm. It was January. "I hope you don't get iced in up there," she said.

Again I had a layover in Cincinnati, or northern Kentucky. Then I fell asleep on the smaller plane over to the Eastern Iowa Regional Airport, waking to random family thoughts.

Uncle Pete was a war hero. This seemed strange now but was true; he had stormed the beach as the Allies invaded Europe, twice being decorated and promoted on the battleground. He had married Prudence in a chapel in California before shipping out, then they had not seen each other for more than a year. He'd sent "Bo" his lieutenant's bar when he was promoted to captain. I still had, come to think of it, Uncle Pete's lieutenant's bar in a small leather box of mementos: my grandmother's gold wedding band, my grandfather's ivory handled fishing knife, my other grandfather's—Tom Northway's—speckled guitar pick, the polished agate ring my father wore.

Uncle Pete and Aunt Prudence had a romantic beginning, then a long steady life together in the same house in the same town all the main years. They had come to our wedding in Louisiana, but we had never been to visit them. I must leave off chiding myself for that now. I was going up. Shades of Luke. In their later, and these last, years as Prudence deteriorated and Pete grew slightly palsied and half-deaf and turned to raising dahlias and other flowers to give to people and churches for their pleasure—the story in the newspaper called him then, this stormer of the beach at Normandy, the "Flower Man"— they grew irritable with each other, disconnected.

Like my father, the first Mark Northway, Uncle Pete McDear submerged his feelings and was not much open to those of others, or so it seemed. You checked your field, gathered your strength, and plowed ahead. Empathy was not an available virtue. This could be hard on mules, sons and women.

And like my father, Uncle Pete drove hard and was of the idealistic, individualistic American breed, believing always in the American Dream until they got screwed— and even then, yes, even then! Pete worked all his adult life for one company, for many years as senior vice president, fully expecting to be president one day, astounded when the young son of the owner took over and they thought it was time for him to retire early, though it was the last thing in the world he wished to do. He found flowers. Except for Prudence's arthritis, osteoporosis and incipient emphysema they might have traveled. Their real world then, as it turned out, was grandchildren, an even dozen of them!

The plane was a little early. Knowing that, though Greg might not recognize me, I would know my large, blue-eyed cousin, I proceeded to the baggage claim carousel, hoping my Lands End bag with funeral suit had come on through. As I took it off the moving circle I saw Greg, smiling, coming to me.

We shook hands. Greg did not condescend by trying to take the old man's bag but said, "Come on, Bo. So good you came. Last time was at Joy's, right? I didn't tell Dad about her. I—"

"I told him over the phone, when I called to say I was coming. It didn't seem to upset him in the context—in the course of things."

Pete Jr. had driven over from Nebraska and was waiting at the car. He was not as tall as his brother but big, solid as a rock, his eyes even brighter blue. He looked like a bigger, tougher Bruce Willis. His hands were rough from outside work. He hugged his long-lost cousin, also greeted me as "Bo."

It had been many more years since I had seen my cousin Pete than since I had seen my cousin Greg. It had been since Pete Jr. as a young man had driven to visit me in Texas in his old Impala. He began at once to share things that "Bo"—that I—had said to him, that "Bo's" father and mother had told him, all the family stories, like a desert hermit drinking from a sacred spring of family, like one washing window panes so he could see through them more clearly. I sensed in this reunion the faith and pragmatism of the minister, the idealistic skepticism and near mysticism of the other. These were a couple of guys, my cousins. Pete Jr. kept turning to look at me with his piercing blue eyes as I sat in the back seat of the Oldsmobile, like he could not quite believe it: his mother, never understood or cherished enough as it seemed to him by his father, had passed away and "Bo," symbol of a larger family, of kinship, of memories, was here.

"There are so many of us we got a suite of rooms at the Residence Inn," Greg said. "Pete is staying there too." Pete Jr. had driven over yesterday in his old Ford pickup. Now his wife and four of his children were coming on in his '80s car. His older daughter was flying in from Phoenix. "Why don't you get a room at the place with us? They're giving us a reduced family rate."

Yes, I thought, that would be good. No use to be stuck off by myself, with no transportation.

"If it's all right with Uncle Pete. He made the reservation."

"We'll take care of it."

They pointed out the Old Mill Run motel as they passed by. It was off the highway down by the dark river.

"He was going to put you there!" said Pete Jr.

"It's okay, it's been redone inside," said Greg.

"Was your dad as tight as our dad?" Pete said. "He wasn't all that tight, was he? But he was authoritarian, wasn't he?"

"I can hardly remember my way around over on this side of town," Greg said, heading for his father's condominium. "We only ever came over here for football and basketball games."

"We used to come over here just to drink beer and get lost," Pete said. "That was a big kick, not to know where you were. That was how we had fun, growing up here."

We parked and walked in to the corridors of the Christian condo building. His had his name on a plaque on the door: *Peter G. McDear.* It took him a long time to come to the door. Then the door opened and he stood there, tall, head cocked like an old bird's, broken beak of a nose, frail, slightly shaking, thin as a leaf.

"I'll be," said Uncle Pete, looking at me with pale blue eyes the color of a frozen lake. "You made it. This is my friend Harry." He turned sideways to show us a small man in his eighties with a bulldog face and suspenders. "Harry lives down the hall."

Harry came forward to touch our hands and nod that this was so.

"This is my nephew Bo," said Uncle Pete. "He came all the way up from Dallas. He came up to represent Prudence's side. Well. Let's get this schedule right. I have set up dinner here, a seated dinner in a private room downstairs for five o'clock sharp. Then tomorrow morning—"

"1 hope my troops get here by then," Pete Jr. said. "They're driving that old '83—"

His father gave him a look as if why didn't they have a better car, like, get 'em here, on time.

"I'm sure they'll make it fine," his son said.

We stayed just briefly, then drove back across town to the Residence Inn. The afternoon was graying over, a little sleet coming down. There was a cheerful flicker of fire from artificial logs in the fireplace of the lobby of the inn. "I thought it would be a good place for all of us to gather, relax, talk, be together," Greg said. "How'd you think he looked?"

*Frail*, came to mind. But, still, with such a sense of authority. I said neither.

"He's really thin," Greg said. "He was in that wreck. That's why we took him with us for a month, and he had to put Prudence in the place. She was disoriented, she didn't know why she was there, alone."

"Who wouldn't feel dissociated," his brother said. "My God."

I realized there was a triangulation of tensions, but they were being kept submerged.

"Jesus, my bunch will never make it here by five," Pete, Jr. said.

Up on the seventh floor, unfolding and hanging up my suit, I went to answer a knock at my door.

A boy seven or eight, blond, blue-eyed, very much a young McDear, looked appraisingly at me and said, "Are you Mo?"

I smiled. The boy had heard "Mark" and he had heard "Bo" and had come up with "Mo." "Sure," I said. "Come in."

"I'm Kirk," the kid said. "I just wanted to see what you looked like. You're our family. They say come on down the hall and be with us. You can hear where we are."

The kid was right. I could hear them, talking, singing, laughing, as I walked down the hallway and into the center room they had with other rooms going off it. Instantly I met a college senior, Kristina, who hugged me. Her mother, Edie, seemed too young to have all these children, trim, pretty, like a mother bird watching her brood flip around her as she made up a book of photographs from the past of Prudence, and their grandpa, and all of them through the years. I found myself in it as "Bo," young, lean, tanned, hair flopping in face, in a pictured circle of my parents and aunt and uncle displaying a string of Great Northern pike caught on our summer trip together to the lake in Minnesota.

And Kristina's brother, attending the same college with her. And the next brother, Kris, a senior in high school and reciter of poetry, and their junior high school sister, and the three brothers down the line, Kirk who called me "Mo" in the middle of them, all with names beginning with "K" or hard "C." It was a blessed gaggle and a merry babble, where I was instant "Bo."

"Hey, Bo." "You want an oatmeal cookie, Bo?" "Bo." "Bo—"

It felt good to be this "Bo" again.


Talking poetry and poets with Pete Jr.'s older daughter who had arrived from Phoenix and with Greg's highschool son Kris—they liked Diane Wakoski and Robert Frost respectively—and walking down to the ground floor private dining room a few minutes late, I, and all of us, found an agitated patriarch.

"They're not far, about fifty miles," Pete Jr. said. "The fan belt broke this afternoon. It was hard to get it fixed on Sunday."

"The food is ready. They're trying to keep it warm. The waitress has come and gone. . . ."

Uncle Pete wore a jacket and a necktie and seemed larger, more erect, even commanding, more the person I remembered. He looked at his elder son, at the flock of his other son all present.

"I'm sorry they had trouble," he said. "I appreciate everybody coming. Let's tell the guy, the chef, we'll be ready by six, six-fifteen? The food should hold till then.

Well." He rubbed his quivering hands together, a bit like Jimmy Stewart in an old movie. "Let's sit down and visit for a while. I think there's a playroom for the little ones down the hall."

"Yes, thank God there is," said Edie.

Before too long the other clan, Pete Jr.'s wife and the rest of his children, arrived in force. They came pouring in, kissing and hugging Grandpa, cousins greeting cousins, all this bunch now also meeting and greeting "the professor," "Bo." They arrived just under the wire, when the waitress was still on duty to serve them and the chicken and potatoes had not gone cold. Greg brought the blessing in the name of the Lord Jesus Christ, and we all sat and ate. I sat at the small round table with my uncle, who said not a word during dinner, and with his sons.

After apple pie the point of the occasion was revealed as Pete pushed himself up and undid the napkin from his neck and looked around and said he wished to say a few words and then he wished for each of them to say something about Prudence, to share her memory, and about the meaning of being a member of this family. He spoke with the slow authority of his years and of being their father and their grandfather.

"I first saw Prudence at a family meeting outside Cleveland at the old Hathaway homestead, an old farm place there. She was a girl, about eleven. I was a year or so younger, you see. The family moved there, to her grandmother's place during the Depression of the Thirties when her father, Judge Whitlock, lost just about everything. Then they moved on out to California, where he was a judge advocate, the first civilian judge advocate, to the Air Force there. Prudence and I were kin already, having some of the same Hathaway cousins, you see.

"Well, next time I saw her she was a young woman, and I had never seen such a beautiful woman. Blond, blue eyes, terrific figure. I thought, 'Oh boy, what a babe!'" He made a clucking sound in his cheek with his tongue, and beamed.

"I was in the service a little later, like everyone else, and we got married in a pretty little chapel in California, and I had to ship out immediately, and we didn't see each other for a good long while since I was on duty in the European Theater with the infantry, and the war, and so forth. Then I came back and we moved to take a job in Saint Paul, Minnesota, and then with the same company, at the head office, here to Cedar Rapids. We had a good and regular life together, I think, and so forth."

Uncle Pete stopped and rubbed his hands and coughed, as if that was about enough of personal history.

"Now you young people should know a little of the history of the McDear family.

"They came to this country and settled here and there, and then the two brothers, my grandfather and his brother, had a creamery business in Ohio, in Twinsburg, but they were wiped out in the Depression of that time, in the middle eighteen-fifties. So they came on out here to Iowa, they'd heard the soil was dark and rich, but the good land was just about all taken up by then. But they found a section up by Nebraska, right on the border there, so they got two hundred and twenty acres instead of the usual hundred and sixty. Being of Scots descent, they thought that was a pretty darn good deal. My grandfather brought some cattle over from Scotland and developed a breed of shorthorn cattle, and they ran cattle there, in Sac County. They worked hard and did all right, and so forth. Then when it came his turn my father got sick and couldn't hold on to it, and died.

"Well, I had to go live with an aunt I hardly knew. My mother had died before my memory, you see. They never told me what happened to my father. I heard them whisper, up behind their hand, that he 'passed away.' I didn't know what that meant. Soon my aunt died, and I was left on this poor farm with her husband, an old man I didn't know much at all, and he didn't know what to make of me. We would sit at the dinner table and look at each other. But I got away and made it all right, and went on to Iowa State, and I studied engineering. Later, after

the service, I got t.b. like my father and went to a
sanitarium in Arizona, but I licked that, and so forth.

"Well."

He held on to the back of the chair in front of him;
but he was not finished. He straightened up and the light
came into his eyes, giving them the intensity I
remembered they used to have.

"You remember I, and some of you guys, were in that
accident. Some of you were here visiting, and I was taking
you bowling, and thank God none of you was hurt. But I
had broken some ribs and didn't know what to do, so I
went over to be with you for a while and had to put
Grandma in a place, it was a pretty nice place, and she
was in and out of the hospital, and she was confused. I
don't blame her. But I didn't know what else to do. I
could not take care of her.

"Then, I was playing bridge with my group for the
first time in months, and I didn't know they were looking
for me, three days ago, and I came back to my place here,
and they said go to the hospital.

"She was in the 'hospice room.' I sat in there with
Grandma, and I held her hand. I think she knew I was
there. And as I held her hand. . . . Well, it was warm,
even feverish at first, then it got cooler, and finally it got
cold. I knew that she was gone. I want to tell you young
ones, if you ever have the opportunity to be with a loved

one and share that experience of passing from one life to the next one, do it. . . ."

"Now."

He said he'd like to hear their memories of Prudence and their thoughts about what it meant to be in the family.

They all spoke, with love, and some with humor, in regard to "Grandma's" great good spirit and funny ways and her laugh and unpredictability, and what she meant to them. I stood and told my story, of "Aunty Pru" my babysitter, and my aunt and uncle's loyalty to our family, and of "Uncle Pete's" being my hero when I was a boy.

Then "Grandpa" seemed content. "Tomorrow morning," he said, "we, the family, will view Grandma at the funeral home at eight o'clock. Don't be late. This was not my original plan, and I don't like my plans changed, but Greg thinks this will be good for all of us. Just remember, when you see her. . . ."

He left the rest unsaid, not wishing to err on theology, or wishing to leave that matter to his son the minister. Greg looked at his brother and at me, and, hopefully, above to the Lord, and led us all in the evening's benediction.

It was more frozen, slicker with ice, early in the morning as we all proceeded in Pete Jr.'s car and Greg's two cars and van to the funeral home.

Some of the children held their breath as they filed in to view the body. Greg presided, telling them this of course was not Grandma, she was spirit now and with God. This was the body she had left behind, but it was good for them all to see her one last time here on earth before the resurrection of the body in eternity. There was remarkable quiet as they filed in and stood in a wedge together and little by little went to view her.

I looked at her. Prudence looked, with her white hair and glasses and closed eyes, in her blue dress, with her pearls on, like a woman of her age. Nothing resonated in me that this was "Aunty Pru." I imagined I could hear her wacky laugh at this joke of death, a little aside of a joke between her and her dear nephew "Bo," but that was not true, I did not really feel her "spirit" here with me; my imagination, I knew, was manufacturing her voice and laugh. I seriously doubted resurrection and an afterlife. Then I looked and saw that Uncle Pete was aglow.

"She looks wonderful, doesn't she?" he said. She looked so much better to him than when he had seen her last, or the times before, the dreadful uncertain times in the hospital when she was pitiful, half deranged and looking ghastly.

He said it over and over, what a great job they'd done, how good and natural and like his beautiful wife she looked, how glad he was they'd had this family viewing.

About two hundred came to the memorial service in the Presbyterian church, many couples and individuals in their eighties braving the icy conditions. I stood by Uncle Pete's side in the receiving line and explained who I was and what I was doing here. A number of these good people paused in the line to tell me who they were and exactly what connection they had to Pete and Prudence, and I saw what I had seen standing in the line after Joy's service, how real their lives had been among so many people I did not know and would never see again.

Tired, I went to sit in a circle of the two sets of McDear children, talking to them. Pete Jr.'s kids and their mother were getting ready to roll. Greg and his bunch would leave in the early afternoon if the highways weren't too bad. Pete Jr. would stay over for a day or two with his dad.

We left the church and went back to the inn. Pete Jr. took his father to his condo across town. The main thing was to keep him from driving on the ice, having another wreck. They had carried him everywhere the whole time. He was stubborn and also forgot to use his cane; he thought he could still do anything.

I went down to the complex of rooms as Greg's bunch packed to leave. It was amazing. Chaos became order as bags were stuffed, boxes packed, clothes and food taken to the cars. The sun was out enough to go. Kris would drive the Olds, Greg the van, Kristina her car.

"It was a good service," I said to Greg. "And your father was truly glad for the viewing."

"I'm glad you'll be here tonight," he said. "Maybe Pete can drive Dad's car and you all can have dinner. I'm glad you came, Bo."

I stood on the walk as they peeled out of the parking lot. Kristina and her brother in her Honda honked going out. Greg and Edie and the little ones in the big Ford van waved and honked. Kris, in the Olds, headset on, honked and waved as he spun on out.

"Goodbye, Bo," he called.

I waved and went in to take a nap.

I woke up to the buzzing of the phone by the bed.

"Say, Bo. Mark. I always think of your father when I call you 'Mark.' Thought I'd come and visit, if you're up and at 'em," Uncle Pete said.

I said, sure, and got up and went down the elevator to wait for Uncle Pete and Pete Jr. to come over from across town. I sat on the couch in the reception area with the gas-log fire providing warmth and a view out the slatted windows to the walkway to the front door. It had grayed over now, gotten colder, refrozen in the later afternoon. I heard a car gun and slip out in the parking lot.

I sat in a warm reverie, thinking that maybe now "Aunty Pru" would come to me, but she did not. Somehow, though, somewhere, I sensed her cutting up, laughing, embarrassing her mother, Remember, with her sisters, my mother and Alma's mother, the Hathaway girls. They seemed, in my mind's eye, to be wearing garb of the Twenties, "flapper" dresses and hats. That was because of the old photograph of them I kept on my dresser at home, of course.

Looking up and through the window, I saw Uncle Pete, by himself, without his cane, walking slowly up the sidewalk to the entrance to the inn. He had driven over by himself. His hand shook slightly and he came slowly, steadily on. I realized that indeed he would, could do anything. He came steadily as he had come through the waves and onto the beach at Normandy. He came in his beaked cap and windbreaker and it seemed to me that Uncle Pete was not only himself coming up the walk but also my father, and my grandfathers, all those who had given me life and relied on me to use it well. I thought that Pete McDear was all the McDears, who had gone bust in Ohio and came to raise cattle in Iowa, and all the Northway men down the line to myself, old "Bo," the last

Northway, coming up the walk to greet and bless me. I went around to the front door as Uncle Pete opened it and came through and smiled at me, his faded blue eyes teared from the cold.

"You came down to meet me?" he said. "That's nice." Upstairs in my room he said, "I am sorry about Joy, your sister, dying like that. She was a good Joe. Well, now. We'll have a talk, get a little more acquainted, see what you think about George W. Bush down there in Texas, and so forth, then we'll call Pete, he's asleep back at my place, and I'll spring for dinner. I like this joint right down the road here, a little chain restaurant, I get a half order of their skillet special, it's a pretty good value. How does that sound to the professor?"

I said it sounded fine.

4.

First came the Millennium and then my big birthday. Gloria gave me the handsome pen I'd always wanted, and I kept it carefully in its box on my desk for now, not wanting to rush into the luxury of using it. My stomach hurting and then nearly killing me, I soldiered through the fall of 2000, but the next term, my birthday term in the spring was a golden one. My intro writing class glowed with talent and enthusiasm. The Hispanic students—Victor, Myra, Sara—and the black students— Monique, Emmit, LaToya—and the Anglo kids— Patrick, Lindsey, Sean, Dan—lifted my Southwestern lit class high with interest and debate so all I had to do was walk in, produce the Silko or the Harjo, the Anaya or the Cisneros and snap crackle pop they were at it, making me feel, dear God, young—like I was walking into fresh new classes when I was beginning, in my twenties, and "with it," and real. My favorite hours in the fiction writing class, being the traditional teacher that I am, were noting the decline of experimental metafiction and deconstructive fiction and decrying the use of melodrama, coincidence, sentimentality and *deus ex machina*, resolving the story by some circumstance or act from outside. They were free to be wooed by the sedulous "chaos theory" as it applied to literature but should beware of randomness that violated the ancient and honorable story form. Story was making cosmos, order, out of chaos. Making a true story came through resolving the relationships among the human beings, the "characters," in it.

"Random things happen," Gloria wisely replied after listening (again) to the assertion. "They happen all the time, 'in reality,' as you like to say."

"Still," I said.

That same term an older student with a blue bandanna around his head came to my office to visit. He looked like he came from the era of the Sixties. His graying yellow hair hung to his shoulders, and he wore hip-hugger jeans. I looked to see if he was wearing shoes or was barefoot.

"I heard you might have known Carroll Hicks," the fellow, Homer, said. I said that I did. He had been a teacher and a dean here years ago. I had read a year or so ago that he had died at an advanced age.

"I want to do a paper on him for my 'Biography and Autobiography' class. He was my teacher, a couple years ago, when I began community college, before I enrolled here. I'm trying to find anyone who knew him here in the university and so far you're the only one I've found."

"Surely not."

"Pardon?"

"That he taught you a couple of years ago."

"Yeah. He was a great teacher. He was a great and wise man. He wrote a lot of books and poetry and stuff like a long time ago. How come, not?"

"He would have been too old. Why, he was in his eighties I'm sure the last time I saw him—frail as a leaf—five years or more ago."

"Yeah. That's him. Dr. Hicks. He had a Ph.D., but he was just an instructor in the community college there.

I was surprised to learn, then, that he was like a bigshot, a dean, here."

"Yes. He was a colorful dean. Some of us kept copies of his memos. They were outrageous. He was an iconoclast—" I looked at Homer, who had a gleam in his eye.

"I know what that means. 'Brann the Iconoclast.' That's me, man! Dr. Hicks encouraged me to write and speak out and express myself. Why I want to write my paper on him. He was eighty-eight then, when he was teaching me. That is pretty old, I guess—but he never seemed that age, you know? He was like vital."

"Why in the world would he have been teaching at that age?"

"Said he had to. He'd made a lot of financial mistakes. Said he had money once or twice but kept screwing up. He was cheerful about it, though, like it was a joke."

I had heard some of that, without thinking about it much, before we had all lost touch with Hicks, except as a "character" in our joint memory.

"That's sad," I said.

"Why is it sad?" said Homer. "I think it's great."

I copied some of the memos for him, which he would not understand, not knowing the university context of the time, and he thanked me for them and the interview and said to let him know if I thought of anything neat and positive about his hero Hicks; but I didn't remember anything more. Now I see Homer on campus and we nod. I thought he might take a course in creative writing, but I see his byline in the campus newspaper and I reckon he is sticking to the facts, strange as they may be.

Then, at term's end and just before we left for our vacation trip early in the summer, I broke my promise to Gloria (again).

I stood up in the university chapel and spoke a memorial for my colleague Andrew Osborne, the church historian.

Gloria went I must say calmly with me to the service for Andy, who was a distinguished scholar-teacher and a good guy, and even complimented me on my part in it. She seemed to understand that despite my vow to her not to do any more memorials there was not much you could do when the fellow's wife asked you to speak about him on behalf of his colleagues and you knew him well and respected and admired him. I thought it went well and that I was able to let a little light in. I found a key anecdote that I thought bespoke Andy's humanity and humility, his grace and humor. Andrew was a happy fellow for all his intellectual and professional weight.

"Oh yes, it went well," Gloria said after the service. "You are a pro all-star memorialist, and I'm sure Edith appreciated it. She sat there wet-eyed with a smile on her face while you were speaking. I'll tell you what you should do, and I would appreciate having it on hand, you should write out your own, with a humorous anecdote or two about how you are losing your mind and memory—"

"I beg your pardon?"

"—and I will keep it handy and give it to the Bishop to read when the time comes."

"Good God, I wouldn't want the Bishop to do it."

"Who then?"

"Someone who cares. Someone who knows me. Someone who will say something true, something real. You."

"Oh," she said, "not I. Like Edith I will be really utterly within myself, and my thoughts of you. As you would be of me. Bathed I am sure in music if not tears. My God, Mark, we are—you are anyway—seventy, can you believe it? Anyway, I forgive you. It was good you could do Andy. Just please, from now on, if you possibly can, stop doing the memorials. I told you, people are going to start thinking of you as a regular Digby O'Dell or whatever his name was. The 'Friendly Undertaker.'"

"I had forgotten about him."

"I know you care," she said.

Sipping merlot, we talked of friends past and present either behind or ahead of us on the trail. We were concerned about a close friend who had been in and out of the hospital without a definitive diagnosis. She and her husband were planning a trip abroad so we figured she would be all right. I said I was looking forward to our little trip, our visit "up in Michigan."

"Makes you feel like young Hemingway, does it?" Gloria said. "You are still a Romantic boy."

I'd written a thesis on Hem's stoicism all those years ago and was about as far away from that as one could be.

I was not too old or jaded not to wonder still at the incredible act of flying. The seats in the 737 were comfortable, even though I was in the middle seat, Gloria by the window and the biggest, fattest man in the plane in the aisle seat by me, the fellow's arms lapping over the seat arm, his odor of garlic and perspiration tickling my nostrils. Captain Anderson announced that we would climb to 36,000 feet, and for all I knew we did. The clouds below were white and beautiful, and we had some turbulence, a bumping and sliding and slight falling out of pattern like we were being rocked in the arms of the upper world. The big man slid around in his seat and seemed frightened and confessed to me that he didn't like to fly. The snack was a cold ham and cheese sandwich that I devoured and a cup of chocolate pudding that Gloria told me not to eat and which I enjoyed thoroughly. For drink Gloria had water, with ice in a cup, and I asked for Coke Classic.

"You don't have to say 'Coke Classic' anymore," she said. "You can just say 'Coke.'"

Later I half -heard her say, "It is amazing to me how you can go to sleep anywhere, under any conditions." I was awake to snuggle up to her and see the architectural wonders, the tall buildings of Chicago—I clearly saw the Sears Tower—and the glimmer of the lake as we landed.

At the rental car lot I chose a full-size Buick like ours at home, and we found the highway through Chicago to the toll road to Michigan. It took two hours at 5 m.p.h. to go from the airport to the Loop. On the toll-way we were following not an old-fashioned map but a written sequence of directions that Gloria had pulled up off the computer. She thought there should be another toll booth before we came to the highway split between Ohio-bound and Michigan. Driving, I looked each way, vacillated, managed to get us dead in the center between lanes, was by some miracle of suspended motion or judgment not clipped by the semi coming by on the left heading to Ohio or smashed by the eighteen-wheeler veering by on the right going full blast for Michigan. Somehow I

straightened out, made the lane, and had in one piece
jumped into the right right lane.

"That was bad," said Gloria. I did not look to see how
white she'd turned.

"That was nearly curtains," I agreed. I had not even
seen the truck on the left coming. For a moment I was
numb, my submerged dread of driving on the highway at
all flashing up, thinking of my sister Joy killed on the
highway, her Explorer hydroplaning and rolling over on
the interstate. I was almost too numb, unnerved, to drive
on. Life was contingent. I had nearly killed us.

"You can go a little faster now. We're all right,"
Gloria said.

God, I thought. You bum. I got the Buick back up to
seventy, seventy-five. We made good time.

We turned off the highway and onto the state road
and then onto the county road lined by trees and acres of
blueberry bushes and turned off the winding asphalt road
into Jason and Michele's driveway, going up and in to the
cottage set right above the massive silver lake just a few
hours behind schedule, when afternoon was ending and
the shade of evening coming on.

"We had a little slowdown from the airport through
Chicago, but then we didn't spare the horses," I said, after
we had clutched and hugged and stared at each other to

make sure we were really here and intact and together in this good place once more.

"Mark has been using these old cliché phrases," Gloria said, laughing, "like from his dad's or granddad's time."

"Well, he always was basically a hayseed," Jason said, laughing too, as we went in the cottage and through it and to the bluff beyond to view the lake, which was pale as ice and absolutely calm.

"I don't think I've ever seen it so calm," I said. There were hardly waves, just rolling ripples. "Have you been in the water yet?"

"Waiting for you. I've seen some kids in down the way, but it's too cold for adults. Of course, the kids get out there on those damn speed jets, whatever you call 'em. Jet skis. I'm sure they're sad to see it calm and peaceful. Let's have a drink, sit out here on the deck. See what a big beach we have this year? Everything has changed and shifted from last summer. Remember all that timber and stuff over there? It's all covered over by sand. But the bluff's held firm. I guess the lake won't get the cottage before we're gone. Scotch?"

"Sure," I said.

Gloria gave me a look but didn't press it. "Red wine," she said. "Any kind of red. We've actually just been drinking red wine. We were planning to stop and get some. We'll go in tomorrow. . . . "

"Don't be silly," said Michele. "We have wine. Don't we, dear?"

"Sure. I get this stuff at a wholesale place in D.C., I think it's pretty good."

We sat out on the deck overlooking the lake paling into twilight and the great round red sun setting over it, no clouds, no waves, and renewed the blessing of our friendship. Gloria and I had first come to this place when Jason and Michele married nearly fifty years ago. Jason had always been like a brother to me, and now with my half- brother Jake and Luke and Joy gone, he was the only one I had left besides Gloria who had known my mother and father, who knew the place where I grew up, who knew who the characters in my early story were. When I met Jason in college, why, of course, we had been just boys growing into men.

He was to me an admirable character. He grew up here in Michigan of an English father and a mother rooted in the culture of the Dutch who had so strongly settled here. Jason had a good small-city life in the town nearby. But his high school counselor advised him that he would never make it in college and he got sent to junior college. But he persevered, and transferred to the college where we met. To make a good story better he went on to divinity and doctoral degrees. He was a lucid and caring teacher and a distinguished expositor and scholar in religious studies. He was a year ahead of me on the trail, had retired a year ago. He was wiry, energetic, humor in his eyes. We always walked along Lake Shore Drive and walked the beach together. The water would be cold, and colder in pockets in the lake, and so by God we put on our swimsuits and went in, a little. .

Jason was thinking and writing about a figure of the last century in the Catholic modernist tradition, a person who believed, as I thought I did, in spiritual transcendentalism but who found no evidence of God in nature or nature's random plan. I found this astounding. In my heart I was, as Gloria had suggested in another context, that Romantic boy who hung out in the library stacks of the college reading Locke and that Wordsworth who climbs to the top of the mountain and looks out upon the vista and beholds his own soul. I had told Jason of Gloria's objection to my doing, falling seriatim into, so many memorials. Now, along the beach, I said, "My main problem with the memorials is that I really do believe in the people—I have to have known the person—and want to give the final gift of his or her identity—but I have to steer clear of offending the literal-minded."

"Yes." He nodded. He had written on myth and metaphor and sacredness in all the faiths, Christianity, Judaism, Islam, the rest; the larger contexts only strengthened his own faith.

"I mean," said I, "I'm really not a believer in any fundamental sense. Don't believe in Heaven or Hell, or the virgin birth, and especially not the grotesque idea of the resurrection of the body. So where does that leave me? Just a damned old humanist, I guess."

"You generally have to believe not just in Jesus the wisdom guy but in Christ to be a Christian," our friend observed.

"Yes, well, it's just a minor problem with the memorials. They are generally held in churches and in chapels. Usually there's another guy, an ordained man or woman, a minister, to take care of that. I'm like the 'color' guy announcing a football game. Bring a sense of the personal, of character, personality, to the audience's assumption of faith. Would a fellow be up there in the church, in the chapel, holding forth, if he didn't believe?"

The Reverend Dr. J. laughed. Then he said, "If I had to do one for Jesus, I'd say, sure, he was a mortal caught in history like all of us, a radical Jewish guy, a great storyteller and parable-maker, a real genius with one-liners, and then so what? For me, and we are all needing to take sides on this, He's in the Gospels and then in all we've needed for Him to be, since. I can believe in that. You ready to turn back?"

I was. My feet were hurting from the hardness and the wet coldness of the sand.

"As for me," Jason said, 'I'd be content to be laid away without words, to let the liturgy, the music, the signs and symbols of the faith do the job. My Lord, I don't need some bozo saying something memorable about me. Even you, Mark. Especially you. Good heavens, you'd tell them college stuff—about my spending nights in the library studying and sleeping—or how we drank so much beer at that isolated college we ruined our kidneys and bladders and ruined our chances to be bishops and college presidents because we couldn't stand for hours in robe and regalia. You'd have the congregation in stitches, wouldn't you?"

Late that night, black with no stars and hardly a sliver of moon, I woke up and got up as the others were sleeping and let myself out the screen door and went back out to the edge of the bluff and sat on a cold wooden chair on the deck and kind of half-saw and half-heard the rippling waves on the lake. The water had remained so strangely calm and clear.

I'd said to my friend, my brother Jason, coming up from our walk on the beach, "Three score and ten fell on me like a cape, like a cape of gold lined with black. The thing about it is, you have to wear the damn thing."

"That's good stuff, Mark, that cape stuff," he said. "It fell on me like a feather in the wind."

"Really?"

"Hell no," he said, bouncing up the metal stairs from the beach ahead of me like a cricket on the hop.

Matthew Arnold was one of Jason's guys. Sitting out there that night between the black sky and the invisible water I felt as "upon a darkling plain." I felt the blackness of the cape of age, felt a bleakness I did not usually travel with.

The next day we picked blueberries and swam and walked again and read and told our stories, and then we had a lovely week with them there on the lake. We had never seen it stay so calm so long.

The drive back to Chicago was a breeze. We navigated downtown and returned the Buick at an underground place on LaSalle. Something on the dashboard said LOW TIRE all the way, but we just kept going. We stayed at the refurbished old-fashioned Palmer House where my father, for a few years a traveling man, had sometimes stayed. In the morning we took the architectural river cruise. I was for the first time at my late age fascinated by how the various architects planned and built the tall buildings on this marshland, sunk them deep and built them tall, fascinated by the sheer physics and engineering of them. How did they know, how could they be sure, that the Sears building could be built so' high as a experiment in construction with so much less steel? It was not like ideas or metaphors in literary stuff that you could get going and fix along the way, I said to Gloria.

"Facts—real things—are not your forte," she said.

In Oak Park we strolled the shady streets after beholding old Frank Lloyd's little structured home and added our stricture. "Wouldn't you have hated to be one of those kids, all packed in together in that one bedroom?" I said.

"All the form followed his function," Gloria said, "then he went off to another woman and left them."

"The second one was the love of his life, of course."

"Yes. Isn't that amazing?"

We had a walking guidebook, but it was pretty easy to spot the Wright and Wright disciple houses among the balloony, bosomy Victorians.

"I like the old Victorians," Gloria said, putting her arm through mine despite the heat that had made us and our clothes soggy on this warm June morning. We peeked in the Hemingway museum a few blocks away, then cut over to the place of his birth, another blowsy Victorian in a state of repair. There a wiry little guide who at first shock I thought might be A.E. Hotchner agilely led us back and forth and up and down the stairs. There was the crib where little Ernest had lain in the bedroom by his sister, next to the large bedroom of his mother, Mrs. Hemingway.

"She was an opera star and a singer, she gave singing lessons, made more money than her husband, who was a doctor. Back then the doctors would make calls," the fellow, who was a pretty deep psychologist, told us. "His room, see, is two rooms away from her, she had the big nice room. If you know what I mean."

"Sent Ernest the pistol his father shot himself with," I said.

"Shh," Gloria said.

On the way back to Chicago in the cab I said, "It's interesting to me that Wright worked right there in a five block area and made a revolution, and Hem went off to make his revolution."

Gloria nodded. "They were both jerks," she said.

That evening we went North Side to a once glamorous restaurant and watering hole that had seen better days. It still glittered with brass and mirrors and photos of the once famous on the walls, though one had to switch back in time, to another age, to recognize those in the photos: Yogi, Leo, Greta, Richard M. I, Ronnie Reagan as a star. There were more folks at the bar than eating at the tables. The bar had a combo and a singer in a shimmering red dress as it must have been in the old days. I imagined Mark Northway, my father, in here. He used to come here for dinner when he was on the road and staying at the Palmer House. Well, the fish and the lamb were okay. The singer did "Sunny Side of the Street" but not "Chicago" of course, that would be too corny, right? The merlot was good. After dessert their waiter-sommelier inquired if that would do it.

"Yes," I replied. "I believe we've done all the damage we can do."

"Why would you say that?" Gloria said. "The poor guy. He's from the Middle East or some place, his English isn't so good anyway. He had no idea what you were talking about!"

Because, I realized, I was thinking of my father, it was one of the expressions Dad liked to use in his array of colloquialisms. It was a strange thing to say. I tried to jolly it off.

"Think," I said, manufacturing a laugh, "if there's a party in here at this table tomorrow night and our guy here comes up at the end, with his big smile, and says to them, 'Well, have you done all the damage you can do?'"

Gloria shook her head. "That would be pretty funny," she said.

*A hairy riot, they used to say. Funny as a rubber crutch.*
*Have you done all the damage you can do?*


Returning home, we found that the house had shifted in the heat already, causing new cracks in several walls. Then, the toilets overflowed, and we found that the kitchen addition a few years ago had been built over our old clay outside pipe that now was cracked and broken at the joints with roots pushing through and holding back the flow of waste and water. How simple it would have been to put in the proper plastic pipe at the time! But I decided not to kill the contractor guy that did it. Who would speak for him? I would simply pray that the insurance adjuster and the special plumbers would say that it would not mean the taking up of all the kitchen floor tile. What bothered us more was that our friend was having breathing problems and was in the hospital for tests. Jack was concerned about her but felt that it could not be anything really serious.

The plumber gang tunneled under my house so it shook and vibrated when I went inside, giving me a headache. It made me think that my image in the bathroom mirror was shaking as I peered at myself. Splashing water on my face I felt that my hands and arms were shaky. I thought of my large, strong, able father, hitting out in anger, as he flapped and shook to death in the grip of his disease.

I went upstairs and found Gloria and embraced her. She looked at me as if she thought I'd gone a little crazy. I said something incoherent about love being the only absolute and went back downstairs and she came down and we stood together with the tunneling going on beneath us.

When our friend grew worse and died in the hospital shortly thereafter, I joined their minister and spoke at the memorial service for her.

## 5.

The new term began in the heat in the third week of August. Storms prowled our prairie and turned the daytime sky black and dark blue, and cracked limbs from our backyard ash trees. We had to have a crew come in and cut up the fallen limbs, which luckily missed wires, and trim the trees; but they said they were not dying and I was glad of that.

We marched to Convocation from my building to the auditorium with its inscription over the doors [Education *Patriotism*Religion] in our robes in the heat and I noticed that mine was indeed the oldest robe—Professor Dunby's had been before he retired two or three or four years ago—after Gloria had congratulated me on its turning such a distinctive shade of browny-green and asked if I'd like a new one for my next birthday. I thanked her and said no. I was proud of the robe's age and sheen, was not about to trade my old friend in. With September came brassy skies and more heat and then in the second week a cool front and powder blue skies and puffy clouds which the planes flew through like silver lances.

Three weeks into the term, on a Tuesday, I had set my class up to discuss the nature of anecdotes and share some of them around the table in my Intro Fiction Writing class, and to discuss the nature of formal dialogue and then the purpose and use of dialogue in stories. I planned to share some key Socratic dialogue in the *Protagorus* and then to offer up Mark Twain's parody of the way it worked in the "Is a cat a man, Huck?" sally between Huck and Jim on the raft.

Nearly forty years before I had been teaching a section of Freshman English and had walked home for lunch and my daughter Glory was a little girl home sick and watching TV and said, "Somebody's shot Kennedy," and I struggled back to campus and we put the flag at half mast and did not know if this was a major attack on the nation or a local idiosyncratic absurdity or just what it was.

Now before I left the house this morning we had the TV on and saw one plane, then the other, absurdly but really, fly into one then the other of the twin towers. It was incredible, and I said I must get to class.

In the Greek-like building, just minutes late, I peered through the doorway into my seminar room. It was a class of fifteen: most of them were there, most sitting silently, a few talking quietly. I found it surreal and walked into the room and without reference to the outer reality (whatever it was) of the attack, began the lesson. Later I learned that a number of faculty colleagues had "discussed" what was happening, (I would not have known what in God's name to "discuss") or dismissed their students to TVs in dorms or the student center. I plowed on with the lesson.

We shared the anecdotes, of family mostly, of "character." I shared some about my grandfathers and about the university. The students participated, not as in a trance but as if in this little cell in this room with blue sky out the window and reality and horror beyond we were in a separate place which for the moment by the power of shared story we were. Some of the stories were funny; once or twice somebody laughed.

Then I could tell they tired of this ruse, this game, the charade, and I gave them, carefully, a dialogue assignment, to write a resolved story all in dialogue, without my addressing dialogue as I had planned, and let them go. They filed out quietly and I must have looked like I felt, crushed into the table, moronic, gone, for no one, as someone usually did, stopped to speak or ask a question.

I had begun to feel strange pains in my arms and wrists about ten minutes before, then a fleeting pain in my jaw. Then a terrible pain not in my chest but in my back like a wire, a hot coathanger, was being pulled through me. Then it went away, and I sat there with a strange numbness and aching and did not think I could get up out of the old split-cushioned teacher's chair at the head of the seminar table. But I got up and staggered out to the parking lot and managed to open the door of the car and drove the short way home. Going in my front door I no longer felt pain, just very odd and tentative. Gloria said something about the terrorists, the situation, and I said I'd had a strange experience but I felt better, I would just take an aspirin and lie down and would probably be all right.

"Lie down and die!" she said. "Maybe you're all right and maybe you're not. We're going to the doctor."

She drove me to my internist in a building near the hospital. He came out and looked at me and shook his head and said, "Why did you come here? You should know better. You should have gone straight to the emergency room. Why, if this had been—Go there now. I'll call ahead for you."

I didn't feel too bad sitting in the emergency room with Gloria. They took me in from there fairly quickly. Drew blood, etc. Young doctor said they couldn't tell from the first test, they would do another enzyme test. They put me in a double room. Separated from me by a curtain was a big well-built guy. He had the raised room TV on mute showing the planes hitting the towers, the bodies falling, the chaos, again and again and again. The human toll and truth of it hit me, uncertain as I was of my own condition and future. As I viewed the large absurdity on the screen I heard the small absurdity next to me beyond the curtain. At first I could not tell what it was as its repetition began to drive me nuts. Gloria came in and said that the guy had a bag of raw carrots. He ate one after another, chomp chomp chomp, chomp chomp chomp, carrot after carrot. He'd had a heart attack. What did he think—that eating carrot after carrot, like a zoo-pent rabbit, would somehow help him now?

In the evening they moved me to a private room, and Gloria went home later in the evening. I was feeling normal now. "Maybe it wasn't," she said. I nodded but thought it had been a redhot wire pulled through my back, had been a very real finger of pain in my jaw.

About ten o'clock the large black nurse came in and said cheerfully, "You had a heart attack, baby. Let's shave your groin."

In the morning the heart specialist said, "Well, sir, you've had a mild heart attack." They went in to do an angiogram and gave me a stent while they were at it. I was out of there in a couple of days and into Cardiac Rehab and felt better than I had before.

It seems, to use the operative word, strange, and to add to it, silly, to have had a heart attack on 9.11, just a tick in terms of the terrible tragedy of the towers and the Pentagon and the loss of the gallant resisters in the crash in Pennsylvania. The horror and courage of that day gripped me and I felt empathic toward those who died and those who survived that day. How could we ever make an adequate memorial for so many?

I felt at the same time a deep need to affirm my own life, and I began to study the photographs of family set out around the room. A photograph showing my grandmother Remember held my eye.

It was a photograph of turn-of-the-last-century students in high collars, vests and ties or shirtwaist dresses looking out solemnly past the camera. They are Hiram College students, in Ohio, and my lovely, clear-eyed grandmother Remember Hathaway Whitlock is in the front row looking serenely into her future. On the back row in the photo, gazing off into the distance from the upper left hand corner, as the caption says, is the "renowned Hiram poet" Vachel Lindsay. Not yet renowned, he appears mesmerized. His and Remember's gazes seem to go in opposite directions but not to intersect, paralleling the relationship as he courted her at the college there. Once the boy with ringing rhythms in his head got as close as the porch of her home in Wabash, where he recited poetry. As the story goes, her parents found him strange.

What I suppose attracted the young poet was her streak of mysticism.

Remember had a mystical bent, as my mother had to a lesser extent. Remember, my mother said, would help those dying to "go across," to cross the boundary from flesh to spirit. Once, standing on the shore of Lake Erie, she heard the cries for help from men drowning in the water off a sinking freighter miles out upon the lake and went to them in spirit. Her daughter Louise, my mother, who nurtured the writer part in me, was a secret poet. I believe now that she was more just sentimental than mystical—though she was a believer in parapsychology in its day and could always "see" what the numbers on the playing cards were held up behind the screen. She did confide to me that she had helped my other grandmother Mattie Northway reconcile her fears and cross over into the realm of the spirit when that time came. And now she comes to me from time to time, as spirits do.

After that experience of the attack upon my heart coinciding with the attack upon us all I was feeling both more mortal and more mystical. I know I am no more

really "mystical" than Gramp Tom's goat Hubert de
Burgh; it's just sharing even more deeply than before
Remember's and my mother's sense that spirits close to
you and passed on, in some very real way we do not yet
understand, remain alive and close to you and can as you
live on, in some way speak to you. I am hearing more
than ever now my father's voice, and my grandfathers'
Luke and Tom, and Luke's and Joy's, as well as
Remember's and my mother's.

Remember and her sister Patience were born in the
1880s on a farm in Independence, Ohio, daughters of the
Hathaway families who were pioneer settlers of the
Western Reserve. They were descendants of John and
Priscilla Alden and of Anne Hathaway and loved to read
and to write in letters and in journals.

"We grew up on a farm, my Beau," Remember wrote
me from her home in California before she went in the
"nursing home." "What was important was basic, shelter
and food and family and fun and human relationships.
My memory of it all is beautiful. I am grateful that after
all the years two fragrances from the old place remain as
fresh to me as yesterday. In our pantry were big yellow
quinces whose aroma was to me so intoxicating that l
would take one and go out and sit on a stump and bite
into it, only to spit it all out. Quinces were not meant to

be eaten like apples. I would go back to get another because I so loved the smell.

"The other fragrance that so delighted me was in Aunt Bea's flower garden, where she grew sweet peas of one color only, big pink and white beauties. How fragrant they were! Honey bees came and sipped their nectar, and it went into honey as delicious as that from the orange blossom or the clover bloom.

"We would drive out," Remember wrote, "in our double cutter and Father's team of bay horses. Long ago as it has been, this drive remains with me in all its charm and beauty. The heavy snow had packed on the roads, so that the sleigh, drawn by those spirited horses, sped along. Everywhere the trees hung with frozen dewdrops, sparkling, prismatic. Everything glistened in the sharp, clear, tingling air, and the jingling bells on the horses made merry music for us. With warm bonnets on and veils over our faces, tucked into buffalo robes, and with wrapped hot soapstones at our feet, Sister and I thought of the glory of the day, of Jack Frost's handiwork, and of the loving welcome at the end of our drive."

The other event in my life most like my heart attack on 9.11 was my grandfather Luke and grandmother Remember coming for my high school graduation and Grandpa Luke dying on the morning of that day. I want to record that now so that there will be no thought that Remember Hathaway Whitlock was a self-deceiving crackpot or a sentimental sap. She was a realist married to a gentle Romantic, and she was a real tough cookie.

Luke and Remember and my grandfather Tom Northway (Mattie having died by then and he gone out to the farm) came to see me graduate. I was winning a class honor and recall feeling pretty cocky. My dad, who was somewhat of a tyrant to us about working around the place, proposed right after breakfast that we "stir our stumps" and get a few tasks done that morning before we all mobilized for the afternoon and evening graduation events. Gramp Tom in his floppy hat went up on the front porch and sat in a rocker and smoked Lucky Strikes, telling his son he had enough tasks to do around his farm, thank you but he would happy to watch and whatever other fools work. Grandpa Luke agreed to trim the long high hedge and went at it with the hedge shears like a house a-fire, his long thin arms in constant motion as he slashed and cut. Dad set my brother Luke, disgruntled, to watering tomato plants while he mowed the side yard with our walking tractor and Remember went down front to tell her Luke to slow down, it didn't need to get all done this morning. She was not pleased with Dad for setting these tasks this day. Mom, inside with Joy doing dishes, was also displeased. It was hot and humid. But my little grandmother sat down at the redwood table on the flagstone patio and asked me to sit and talk with her. Dad had not directed me to do anything because it was "my day."

We talked of Grandpa Luke and my love of the various stories he had always made up and told to me, and of the times he'd taken me fishing on our family vacations on the lake in Minnesota. She spoke of her love of Dickens and asked if I was serious in my idea of being a writer, saying that there were enough characters in our family—pointing clockwise to my father and grandfathers at work and at rest—to make up several books. She talked of their recent move to California, "starting up again" in their sixties. A lawyer and former judge in Ohio, Luke was going to be a civilian judge advocate for the Air Force and she was proud of him for taking up a new challenge, deep as their roots went in "our Ohio."

She took my hand and read my palm, saying for all I was born tiny and half-sighted I was a lucky boy. Then she said, "All right, my Beau, I'll let you go. You go help your grandpa. They shouldn't exert so soon after eating. It is too hot for all this working. Your father, good husband and father that he is. I am afraid, is some kind of a fanatic about it. The only worse one in the family about 'getting something done around here' is your Uncle Pete

McDear, married to my Prudence. My Louise and Prudence have a lot in common in their men."

I went down the yard to the hedge.

He stopped chopping at the hedge, the clippers hanging down from his long arms. He let them drop and pulled a bandanna from his pocket and swabbed his face. A cigarette hung from his lips. He stepped back to examine his work, breathing hard.

"Take a break," I said. "I'll go get you some lemonade. It's too damn hot." Sounding to myself adult.

We talked a moment, then he grimaced and slowly sat down in the grass in front of the high hedge, his knees folded up in front of him, rubbing his stomach. "Whew," he said. "I feel funny."

Then he winced and bowed his back, sitting holding his stomach now with both hands.

I ran up the lawn to the house, meeting my grandmother at the front door. Gramp Tom, sitting in the rocker, said, "What?" "He says he feels funny," I said to her.

She looked down to where he sat. Her eyes blazed so blue they looked like she could see through him and the hedge to infinity. "Go get your mother to make some hot tea," she said. "Get it quick." Then she called out "Luke!" and went running down the yard, a small woman with white hair flying, pausing just an instant to kick off her shoes, that strange piercing look in her eyes as if she already knew.

When the emergency people came and pronounced him dead I yelled at them, no, bring him to, and my father like a bear in his old flannel shirt had to hold me back from attacking them as they took him off in the ambulance. I thought I could not bear being in my father's arms in that moment.

Somehow we all managed to get to my graduation later that day.

Back home after the ceremony, I went into the room where Remember was sitting alone. "Going off to your party now," she said.

"I'm not sure I feel like going."

"Fiddle! We all went to your graduation. Go on."

"Do you think that his spirit is still alive?"

"Why, yes. Certainly. Didn't you feel that he was there, with you, when your name was called? Now go on to your graduation party."

Remember passed on in her eighties in a nursing home in California, near her oldest daughter (besides Aunty Pru and my mother) who lived there. Except for her daughters Remember forbade visitors in her last years. She didn't want us to see her old and ill. It was hard for me to obey the order, but now she remains in my memory as vital, fierce and beautiful.

Towards the end she wrote: "Beau—Trying to enjoy each minute now—this A.M. a brilliant male Oriole, flaming orange and yellow, landed on the hummingbird feeder outside my window. He managed to get some of the syrup, too—almost standing on his head to do it— Wish you could have seen him—"

Prudence—Aunty Pru—visited her in her last year, and wrote me that they found the dust jacket of my first book in her bedside drawer and that she had told the nurse of her grandson who was a teacher and a writer.

My father went several rounds with his debilitating disease and died on a morning while I was teaching a Humanities class. I'd gone blank on the Socratic dialogue in that moment and stood looking out the classroom window at a line of live oaks on the campus. I held a memorial service for him in the chapel, and one later for my mother.

My grandfather Tom Northway, who had told me of how his life was given purpose by going out to the old family farm, died there on the farm at ninety. He was planning to plant new fields of flowers and berries in the spring.

So. That was enough of that for now. I got up from this reflecting and turned off the light in the memorial room and went down and had a glass of good red wine

with Gloria, and in the morning I returned to campus
and my classes.

# MESOPOTAMIA

In the late summer before my senior year in high school my family received a letter from my father's father, Tom Northway, who had retired to an old family farm three years before when his wife Mattie died. The letter told of the homely details of bringing the several hundred acres back to life and ended with what Gramp Tom assured us was Mr. Lincoln's favorite poem.

> *Oh, why should the spirit of mortal be proud?*
>
> *Like a fast-flitting meteor, a fast-flying cloud,*
>
> *A flash if the lightning, a break of the wave,*
>
> *He passes from life to his rest in the grave.*

"That's real comforting," my Dad said.

But it made me want to visit Gramp Tom. He was in his seventies now, and I wanted to be with my old story-telling pal. My father, who had just come back from a job interview in Chicago and did not seem happy about it said okay. He seemed to understand why a fellow might want a break at summer's end.

I took the train to Cleveland, and my grandfather met me at the Terminal. We piled in his old Dodge car (with F-Fla-Fluid Drive, as he never tired of pointing out), and drove out of the city into the country, Tom Northway bellowing bits of "B- beautiful Ohio," going towards "the land between the rivers," the fertile valley of Jacob, the rich land where the old farm place lay. We drove through the trading town of Middlefield, slowed down through the village of Mesopotamia and turned into Gramp's road. All the names on the mailboxes along the road except for his were Amish, names like Zooks, and Miller and Mullets and Millers and Zook. Carefully passing a slow black Amish buggy, Gramp pulled into his driveway.

I saw again the snug stone and wood house he'd built with the help of his handyman Big Bill Williams and his Amish neighbors who had quarried the stone from the old Northway quarry and who sugared his maple trees for the syrup. The stout block outhouses, the granary, the barn, a century old and half sunken in.

When they lived in Cleveland, in Shaker Heights, Mattie had never let him have more than a canary in the house. Now his English bulldogs Jiggs and Jill came wagging and slobbering to us and his milk goat, for some reason that escaped me named Hubert de Burgh, came walking dainty-footed to us. She nuzzled her head on Gramp's leg and munched the Lucky Strike he produced for her.

"Well, here it is," he said. He looked out over it, white thatch of hair under floppy hat, belly protruding over his worn jeans, and lit a Lucky of his own. Then he began a story, this not a joke or an anecdote but a serious one.

"When Mattie died, and your father and you drove all night to Cleveland there to help me, you remember I am sure that I disappeared, upsetting you all terribly. And, Bo, you were the one who found me sitting in the car in the garage there, this same old car, which is why I keep it running and do not get a new one. Well, I truly thought that with Mattie gone—she ran my life, you see—my life was over then. I knew I could not practice dentistry anymore.

"So I went a little crazy. You remember I gave all the silver and linens away to the cleaning woman, but your father, of course, he went and got them back! I pretended I was all right, then, but I felt as if I was slit in half, inside.

For the only time in my life I did not wish to live. I saw no point in it.

"But when we had buried her and you had left, and I was just terribly all alone—except for that damn bird of hers singing in its cage in the solarium of that s—staid house—for some reason I will never logically understand—some voice, or force, was directing me I now realize—I came out here to this old, r-ruined place that I had visited so often as a boy. It was nothing but weeds and wilderness. Uncle Ed had long since passed on, he was the last of the Northways to have farmed it. The Amish had moved in all around, and made the colony they have here. Uncle Dan, the executor, had sold off hundreds of acres of the old place—my God, at one time it was eight square miles of Northway land! Sold it to the Amish, these very fine farmers who live here now.

"I came out, in that Dodge car, in the evening, up from Cleveland. I drove so slowly, in a trance, that the cars behind me honked at me constantly. And right there—" Gramp raised his strong arm in its checkered flannel and pointed. "—by that h-huge gnarled apple tree that does no longer bear, I found a leafy spot on that spring night and I lay down there, utterly alone except for the presence I began to feel with me of the Great Father of Us All and I said to myself, Tom Northway, you fool, you have mostly sat out your life and s-suppressed your real j-joys and talents, your time is past, here is a good place to be at rest, to pass on."

I watched and listened as my grandfather threw his shred of tobacco away and Hubert de Burgh came quickly to scarf it up.

"But then, when I woke up, stiff and sore, the sun was out, it was a marvelous morning. A red squirrel was sitting by my feet, with a nut in its paws, chattering at me like M-Mattie used to, telling me to do this and that, and in that moment of awaking I knew there was something in life more for me to do right here, and I asked God the Father for my life and health and sanity, and I s-stood up and brushed the leaves off my clothes and the cobwebs from my head and began to do the work here that it had always pleased God for the Northways to do.

"Isn't that interesting? Well, Bo, do not stand there like a dunce. Come inside, and I will fix you a feast that city folks cannot match!"

The feast was spuds and beans and carrots from the garden that he rinsed and set to boiling on the stove. "Do you prefer buttermilk or goat's milk?" he boomed. I was hard driven to the choice.

"Two nights ago I spied a doe from here, right there at the edge of the woods. But she didn't bother the garden, just then anyway. How is your father, my son?"

"He's about had it with the television station, I think. I think he wants to move on. He went to see about some big-time merchandising job in Chicago, but didn't tell us what happened."

"I do not think he would leave Ohio. He loves that place of yours."

He began to chord and sing as I listened to him and the sound of crickets and night creatures and smelled the cooling earth. He sang "Duck Foot Sue" and "Boarding House in Manaway," the old comic songs that I had heard him sing so often. I asked him if he had made them up and he said, no, they were passed down in the family, Uncle Ed used to sing them years ago sitting on this porch. I said I did not remember certain verses that he sang. "Well, if you mean that last one, I didn't remember the ending of it either, so I just made up that 1-last verse."

That surprised me. "Can you do that?" I said.

"Why, h-hell yes," he said.

In a while he said, "To us, your family, Bo, you have been a special boy. That is because you were born in a terrible time, when none of us had a penny, the damn Depression, and you were our first, child and grandchild. And you were born premature, a tiny chap. Your Grandpa Luke said upon beholding you in your incubator that you looked like a little Bohunky (tho' Luke always claimed it was me said it when we went together to the hospital to get a look at you) and that is why we call you 'Bo.' The doctor told Mark, your father, that you could not possibly live, so he named you for himself and of course you did live, and—and then took you home and we all—your mother and father and Luke and Remember and your Aunt Prudence who was just a girl and Mattie and I—cared for you. And so my dear boy I know you will remember as you consider your life and its purpose, that the Great Father allowed you to stay in this life and take your place in it."

Then he said, standing, putting the guitar down, preparing to go and pee by the gnarled apple tree and to let the dogs and the goat into the house for the night, "There is a slight smell of rain in the air. I hope not, for I had planned for us to go in to the B-Bloomfield auction in the morning."

The next evening he told me again the story of the battle between the Great Ram Slugger and the Vicious Dog Hobo. It was one of his "Forty Acres" stories that he liked to tell and tell again. The stories had to do with a character much like himself named Ab Gerry, a shrewd, kind, fat horse trader and his adolescent son Ed and all the country characters who inhabited an innocent, bucolic world of his imagination. He told it at length and with relish and with a few changes from what I recalled hearing before. When he finished I said, "How come you don't write them down?"

"I wrote down 'The Great Ashtabula Train Disaster.' I sent it to you. It is history. This other is a telling story."

I asked if he would mind if I tried to write down the story he had told, to have and to preserve it for posterity. He said sure, it was no skin off his posterior. He knew I wanted to be a writer and this might be good practice. I worked late that night after he and the dogs had retired writing out the story in my notebook as I heard my grandfather's voice telling it, then going back over and correcting it. I have it here before me now: "The Fight Between the Vicious Dog Hobo and the Great Ram Slugger."

It began: *One day when his father Ab Gerry, who owned Forty Acres Stables was away on business, young Ed Gerry heard a mighty argument in progress as he approached his father's barn.*

*As Ed entered the barn he saw it was between Tim McFole, son of Erin, six foot four and thin as a slat with beady black eyes and long black hair that cascaded over his collar, and a small, almost dwarf man who stood perfectly still as if listening to a lecture. His mild watery eyes and bald head, short arms and baggy trousers made the contrast ridiculously funny.*

*A small crowd surrounded the pair as Ed slipped in to hear what it was all about. The man on the receiving end was Dutch Potts. He moved slightly in his number 12 flat-heeled boots—once or twice he even started to interrupt the tirade—but the burst of words continued.*

*"There are dogs and there are dogs," yelled McFole, argument in his bloodshot eyes, his quivering fingers gripping a black stogie. His grimy fingernails were spread like the talons of a hawk and his voice pitched high as he leaned forward as though about to spring. "Some of 'em are trained and some of 'em don't need no training. My dog, Hobo, is a natural fighter. He'd rather fight than eat beef any day. There's nothing on four legs can lick him!"*

*"Look 'ere," said Dutch. "For someone so full of wind as you be methinks you make a big noise. I don't keer one little damn what your dog has ever done or what he has licked. It's money what talks and that's what's talking right now." Dutch reached in his pocket and produced a handful of silver.*

*"Here's fife dollars. It says that Ab Gerry's black ram Slugger can lick the hell out 'er your dog. Now put up the money or shut up. I've had enough of your wind."*

*Even the gray donkey in the stable was at pains to avoid the black ram. Slugger had an evil eye and curving horns, and a head that he used to batter down whatever obstacle obstructed his plans . . . .*

Gramp read it through slowly and said that my handwriting was pretty good but I should take advantage of technology and type it up using his old Oliver typewriter on which he composed his many letters to us. He complimented me on my ability with grammar and syntax and allowed that the story looked pretty good set down, written out, but he himself would continue to tell it without reference to this written version, so he could change it as he wished, lengthen it or shorten it according to the occasion.

"You s-seem to have changed it, I think it is the language," he said. "Why, you have made it as much yours as mine. 'F-froth-flecked, quivering jaw'—I would not say that, I would just say 'quivering.' But I think you have done a fine job of c-capturing it."

It made me happy. I stood out on the porch looking over the farm, thinking of this real farm place and Gramp's made-up "Forty Acres." I saw the dogs chasing after something in the field and the goat dainty-footing towards them. When Gramp came banging out the screen door behind me I turned to him and said, "Where did you get that? Hubert de Burgh. That name for your goat."

Suddenly, like a boy, a toy, I felt myself picked up in Gramp's powerful arms and dangled in the air as he marched to the barn to feed his great horse Rock while giving me a painful "Dutch rub" on the top of my head with the knuckles of the hand that was not pinning me.

"Yowl" I yelled. "Quit!"

"Hubert de Burgh?" Gramp laughed as I struggled in his grip. "Why, I am surprised my great writer grandson does not know that!"

At the end of my visit he showed me, and later gave me, a diary of 1865 that his father Elijah Northway had kept after he came back to the farm from the war. He said there wasn't much to it, just what was done from day to day, but maybe my imagination could make a story out of it one day.

# THE CROSSROADS

That was the year just after I came back home here to Ohio. I'd had my own place before I went off—I had been teaching in the school there from the age of seventeen—and I just came back to it. I couldn't teach that year, and I didn't see how I ever could do it again. It was a blessing I could just come back and do my work and hire out and live through those days, chopping and drawing wood and doing chores and making stools and a plank cable for some neighbors and later in the spring and summer selling some berries and some sweet cherries in to town.

The first time I went out into the woods I could hardly lift the ax.

It was a cold winter, that winter of '65, then it came a glorious spring.

My brother Eli died early in that year. He died Jan. 5 and we buried him Jan. 6. There were four of us brothers that went out from here in '61 after the call came for volunteers. Eli and Ed were older and they went first. They joined up with Capt. Barrows in the 15th Independent Battery Light Artillery and then Elmer and I joined a little later, got in a different outfit and fought a little different pattern, you might say. Ed was the first one of us had a place over by Mesopotamia among the Gentle People. My place then was near our parents' place where we all grew up, by Orwell.

Ed stayed with the 15th and was with Gen. Sherman all the way. He marched "from Georgia to the sea" with that bunch. Eli was wounded pretty bad outside Vicksburg there. The hospitals and the medical attention weren't so good then, most of the doctors I saw couldn't cure a case of warts. Eli made it home but he never did recover right. I went to his funeral at 12 o'clock Jan. 6. Rev. Mr. Leake preached the sermon, on the xxii chapter of Revelations, verse 14. He was buried in the graveyard of the Methodist church. He was a gay fellow who liked to sing and tell stories, like all us Northways. I went home with Elmer that day and stayed all night. The other three of us lived through it, by God's grace, and in my case with a little unexpected help. I was the one went to prison.

I visited regular that winter with Miss Georgeanne Turner. She was a teacher in the school there, and I had known her before. Her father had died and I went to help them some around the place. She had a fine singing voice. I heard her singing that first time I went and helped get a load of wood and chop it into stove wood at the door. I went home and wrote a song for her. She was a plain girl, as I see her now, but when I came back she was more beautiful to me than the rose in all its splendor. I was in love with her. We talked some, sitting in her house there—it would be cold as the devil outside, and snowing like fun, and we would be together snug as two bugs by the fire while she knitted something for the sick. She made my heart lift up again and led me to talk about it a little. "Come out of your dark cave, Lige," she said to me. "For soon it will be spring. You have your whole life before you now."

I took to writing her poems that I never showed her. They embarrass me now, but then I thought them gems. I wrote her poems like:

> *Dare I presume to snatch the nectar'd kiss,*
> *Will you approve of liberties like this?*

And:

> *Say lovely fair, will you agree*
> *To love none else in truth but me?*

But I never snatched it, and she of course could not agree when I could not get up the gumption to ask her.

Anyway, in Feb. I got some bark and bottomed a chair for her and cut some sticks for some handsled runners and sawed them out and made her a sled and we had some good sleigh rides to Hart's Grove together.

On days when it was stormy and snowed and blowed like fury I carried her back and forth to school.

But it was the talking with her that helped me.

Now late in that same spring Abe Lincoln was shot. He was shot on the evening of April 13 and he died at one o'clock next day. On April 19 I and Elmer went to town for his funeral even tho it was a busy time, and came back to Elmer's place and drawed two loads of dirt. On April 28 the President's remains were there in Cleveland, but we didn't go to view them. We always liked old Abe, in Ohio, and voted for him. He was a rough, funny fellow and a sad, burdened one, and he stood against one person owning another, which thing God never intended, and he stood for the Union. I don't believe that Ed or Eli, even at the end, or Elmer or I ever hated the Rebels, even when we were fighting them. God knows, they thought their cause was right even tho it wasn't.

That was pretty much all there was to it when the President's call came in '61 for 300,000 volunteers, None of us was particularly happy or excited about it, or thought of ourselves as patriots. But we figured we must go. As the fellow said, armed Rebellion had reared its ugly head and nobody paused much to ask why.

Like I say, Ed and Eli were some older and got Father's permission first and got the jump on Elmer and me and joined up with Capt. Burrows as gunners with the 15th Light Artillery. They went to Cleveland first, then joined right up with Sherman. We all got together for a reunion, later, at Vicksburg. The Western gang was all there together, at that siege, I can tell you.

That was the cat's-eye, taking Vicksburg, opening up the river, cutting them in half. It was the big marble for U.S. Grant. Then he got his due from old Abe and got together with that red-headed Ohio tiger and they pretty much had 'em then. Ed and Eli were in on that but, as I say, I sat it out,

Ed and Eli went off in Dec. '61 but it was Sept. '62 before Elmer and I were set to go. At that time there was nothing forming up around as. We got permission from Father then to travel down to Cincinnati and joined up with a bunch of Hamilton and Butler County boys that were forming into the 83rd Ohio Volunteer Infantry. We were mustered in at Camp Dennison there. T.B. Skinner, A.O. Hubbard and Gus Hill were also along with us from our county. Gus Hill came back and has remained a friend. He was a brave and uncomplaining soldier, third cousin to us and nephew to our Uncle Zeb.

So the 83rd became our unit, they called it the Greyhound Regiment and we started in to having fun right from the first.

First thing we knew the Confederates under Gen. Kirby Smith were waltzing around across the river in Kentucky and we were sent over there to discourage them from Cincinnati, which was in some panic. Nothing much happened, and pretty soon old Kirby Smith did a Lancers back in his own direction. That was pretty country, with the blooded horses and white fences.

It was '63 before we did too much in the way of fighting Rebs. We were part of the army under Sherman then and of course they waited until winter was coming on and sent us down the Mississippi. We got pretty close to Vicksburg that time, near 30 miles they said, and saw a little action. We burned a bunch of cotton bales at a railroad bridge on a scary big black river there. We fought at a place called Chickasaw Bayou and then crossed the Mississippi R. at a place called Bearsburg or something like, and then moved on to come in some way around behind Vicksburg. What I remember from it is mostly stench and bad water, horses and other poor creatures lying putrid in the streams, and a lot of dysentery, including in the uncharmed bowels of Elijah Northway.

Also the rations ran low so we ate green corn we foraged for days around that place. Anyway, we took Vicksburg, or someone did. Eli was wounded there.

My memory of what we were into then is pretty much like the other fellow's. What good water you could find, you drank it. What we had to eat was salt pork and bread and coffee, no vegetables or fruit. That was hard on an Ohio boy. Many a time I would have given a dollar for a good Ohio apple. I dreamed of picking a bagful of chestnuts, grapes and apples off our place. Later, down in Louisiana, it was worse.

Pretty soon in hot, steamy August the 83rd moved into Louisiana and we marched up along the Teche River there to New Iberia, La. That was where the Acadian people lived. That was—Lord!—about the softest, prettiest country in the world. I was sorry to see us burn it so. But we were under old Baldy now. Anyway, pretty soon we got to New Orleans, and camped at Madisonville, for what seemed forever, considering the people were not what you might call hospitable.

What I remember then was, it was so dull. You could get the Cincinnati *Commercial* there for 5 cents and that saved my life, for I liked to read. I had a volume of Shakespeare from Mother that I carried and I must have read *Hamlet* and *MacBeth* 20 times. I got into a quartet with some other boys and we sang about hanging Jeff

Davis to a sour apple tree and the other usual songs. The Cincy boys liked to play baseball and we did that and raised a little Ned to ease the boredom there in camp. We wondered what in thunder they were saving us for, and before long we found out.

Gen. Banks was getting up a force of 20,000 to 30,000 men, and a gunboat navy, and we were all going up north, they said, in Louisiana and strike over into Texas and capture the whole West away from the Confederacy and grab the Texas cotton. It sounded like a good idea, tho we hankered to be back with Grant and Sherman where the real fun was going to be. The most of Banks' boys were high-pockets, bandbox Eastern dudes. Our little trip was called the Red River Expedition. A.J. Smith, they said, and Ransom, Vance and Emerson, our generals, were fuming, so pleased to get stuck with it, and stuck with Banks, who had about as much capacity as it turned out for generaling as Uncle Zeb's old wall-eyed mule had for courting in the springtime.

So we set out, the whole big army of us, about mid-March of '64, moving up through Louisiana heading for Shreveport, to invest Texas and take that cotton for the Union.

We had proceeded up, last day of March, along the river road to Nakatosh, La. In a few days then we were camped at a place called Pleasant Hills or Pleasant View.

It was pleasant enough, except there was no good water. They said the gunboats were coming up the river, too. Those gunboats were like the dragons in the fables to us, like Santa Claus or Unicorns. They were supposed to join us somewhere, or we them, but never did. For all I ever knew then or now, the swamps and bayous ate them up. So we fiddled around that Pleasant place a while, waiting for N.P. Banks to get his sword buckled on right, or whatever it was that he was doing.

It didn't matter much, the word was. This would be a piece of marblecake. All that was between us and Shreveport and on to Texas was a motley bunch of old men, young boys, Indians and some untrained Texas militia. Old Zach Taylor's son, they said, was in command of this bunch. That was interesting to me, for Zachary Taylor had been a President. His son was a Louisiana man, some said he would fight for it. I was Sergeant Major by then, Company D. 83rd Ohio. You had to figure, I proclaimed in my wisdom, that Dick Taylor would yield back when he saw us coming. Bandbox Banks or not, we had 20,000 men, it looked like more wagons than troops, and a fine jingly bunch of cavalry, even tho that was under a Gen. Lee, no kin we trusted to the other one.

Well, we sat there a while at Pleasant Hills. On April Fool's I remember I put salt in Gus Hill's morning coffee and he drank it down and then howled and danced around, and that was the last bit of fun I had for seven months. On April 7 old Banks figured the moon was right, I guess, and we set out heading slowly over west. Gen. Lee was up front with his cavalry. Then came his wagons. Then a brigade of infantry, you see. Then these wagons the 83rd had. And so on, for miles back. Elmer had been transferred to the 56th Ohio when they got low on men, so he was miles on back, why he got away later on. That arrangement of the troops, then the wagons on back, was what did us in, of course. You won't hear me giving much praise for the generaling of our forces that day.

About noon or some time after noon the column halted. Word came back that the Rebs were up there. Lee's cavalry had come on quite a sight, at a crossroads up ahead. It was called Sabine Cross Roads, and so gave its name to the battle. It was Goodbye, Columbus then, or good bye, Texas, anyway. Orders came pretty soon for the 83rd to detach from the damnable wagons. They marched us up to the front there, several miles it was, I mean quick. It took about two hours of fast marching. They got us into some woods way over on the right side of the line of battle. Then about four o'clock it began.

It was dense forest there, but we could see through it across a clearing, and then the Graybacks commenced to come across at us all up and down the line. They moved the 83rd out of the woods to meet them, and we formed a skirmish line there in the open. The ones coming at us charged running like crazy men. They were a good-looking bunch, with gray uniforms with red and yellow facings. Some of them wore plumes or feathers in their hats. Mostly they were a fine-looking bunch, tho down the line there came a wild crowd of fellows some without any uniforms at all. Whatever they looked like they all meant business and came whooping and yelling across at us, and we held fire and then let go at 200 yards. The first line fell apart back on their second line, then they all came again, and we mowed them down. A lot of Gray boys died bravely in the charge. I was firing lying down by then to avoid the line of fire.

The actual fighting wasn't much but a piece of work when you got into it. It simply started, that afternoon at that crossroads, and you got into it, like chopping wood or making a chair, making the strokes or fittings. You didn't think about it once you got into it. You fired off your piece at something coming at you, making the ramrod do right, thinking really about crazy little things you'd done or a dinner or a good bunk when you were through, just like you thought about little things of your life when you were back home doing chores. That was how it was even with the yelling and the smoke and noise all about.

The Rebs fell back after that first charge awfully cut up. It was brave folly to charge across like that. Later, when I got to prison camp, they said we had killed the Governor of Louisiana in that charge. Whoever we killed, these were brave men, and braver, wilder in a little bit.

Some fat colonel came puffing up to order the 83rd over to the other side. We'd held where we were but there was holy hell over to the left. We could hear the fierce firing all along the line as we passed.

When we got over there, to the extreme left, there was nothing much there at all. The line there had broken, we got over too far, or something about as terrible as it could be, and there we were, as we came out of the woods there to a fence and a clearing, in a pocket. We were outflanked on both sides of the line. At that moment all the Ohio boys knew was that we were in a pickle, and a damn sour one at that.

They were coming at us from the front and from the right, where our own boys should be. We had it hot then there. My hands became blistered from the rifle. Our Captain fell. Then our young lieutenant. I would reckon more than half of us were killed fighting by that fence. I saw the brigade commander, Gen. Vance, come running up to us. One minute he was waving his sword, the next he lay wounded on the ground. Some of the men got back into the woods. It looked like the whole line up to the right was collapsing. Later Elmer said it did, for sure, tho he was with A.J. Smith's men back down the road; they got out of there and rallied back hard then a day or so later. But as for us--

Well, just as our officers who were left were telling us to get out of there—how many I don't know, whatever was left of the several companies of the regiment—here came from the left and from the right a howling horde of the meanest looking outfits, all in rough clothes and every kind of hat and no uniforms at all, cursing and yelling terrible yells. They fired into us until we hugged the ground, firing still, and then they were on every side of us. I prayed then to the Great Father of Us all and knew that this was it. I remember praying with my eyes closed, laid out down by the under rail of that fence that was shot to pieces now. Then when I opened my eyes I was looking right at this fellow in a slouch hat with bright blue eyes and a kind of loose butternut shirt and leather breeches on. He had a revolving pistol aimed at me big as a cannon and he kind of smiled, not looking mean at all but smiling like a happy demon with those blue eyes and that gun on me and said: 'You ready to surrender, Yank?"

It surprised me, for I had never given a thought to surrendering. I was certain in that first moment when I opened my eyes that he meant to dispatch me to Kingdom Come, and why he simply stopped at the fence and asked me so reasonably I will never know.

Judging the alternative with the perspicacity that has always marked us Northways, I let go of my rifle and replied, "I believe so."

"Well, get up then," he said, "and put your hands behind your head and we will keep you safe for Mama."

I obeyed, got up and looked around. Gen. Vance had struggled up and raised one arm like he was about to preach. There were about a hundred of us left alive in a circle who hadn't made it to the woods and were like lost lambs still down by the fence. We were surrounded and surrendering to this wild shaggy bunch.

"All right boys. Gather them up," one fellow said who seemed to be in charge tho he had no more uniform or insignia of rank than the rest of them, They gathered us up, those who could walk, and regular herded us over the fence. I stepped over T.B. Skinner's body following the command. They walked us a mile or two on back, to the west, some way behind their line. Then they let us sit down in a field where flowers were growing in the shade of trees. My captor, with his hogleg out, matched along beside me all the way, as if I was his very own Yank. Over by the little field were tethered a lot of horses, making me figure these unusual soldiers normally were cavalry. Some

guards, in the same casual a
rifles held in the most unmilitary fashion.

Grateful for the shade and for my life but dejected in my spirit, I sat there on the ground. In my young heart I wished I was at least badly wounded or had some good excuse for this.

My captor, the blue-eyed fellow, came over and sat down by me in the grass and picked a stem and looked at it and then at me.

"Got any tobacco?" he said.

I nodded. Northways always have tobacco. I handed him the plug. He brought out a blade and cut off a chew.

"Where you from?" he said.

"Ohio," I said, tho I wasn't going to tell him what my outfit was.

"Well, you bluebellies just got beat back there," he said. "You didn't think we'd let you just walk in and take Texas, did you?"

"Maybe," I said, to both propositions. "Who are you?"

"Bob Campbell," he said, reaching out his hand. It startled me, I had meant to learn his unit. I had never contemplated shaking a Rebel hand, but then I had never contemplated surrendering either. So I shook his hand. I thought he and his irregulars must be some of the Texas Rangers we had heard about so I asked him if he wasn't.

"Ye-ah," he drawled. "Walker's Brigade. We were in the first charge. Then came around to flank you there. Old Tom said your general couldn't lick spit. Look there, there's Tom now—"

A fine old man in a big Western hat came cantering by, stopped a minute on the road near us to sit his horse and look at the prisoners in our field.

"Howdy, Tom," Bob Campbell called.

The old man waved to him. "Howdy, Bob," he called.

"How's she going, Tom?" Bob called.

"Good, Bob," he replied. "Goin' good."

He cantered off, back towards where the action was.

"Tom Green," Bob said to me, with pride. "Old Tom brought us over here. He was a gunner boy at San Jacinto."

I shook my head, not knowing what that was, tho I made a point to look it up later so that I might understand the pride with which my captor spoke of his general.

"Now," Bob said in a little while, "did you see that fellow setting his horse back yonder as we came by, big black horse, his leg throwed over the saddle, smoking that cigar, cool as you please?"

I nodded.

"That was Dick Taylor." Bob got up.

"Good luck, Ohio," he said. "I guess I better transfer you Yanks over and get back up there. We mean to chase you all the way back to where you come from, you know,"

"Where will they be taking us?" I asked.

"Oh," he said, "over into Texas. It won't be too bad."

I will always remember those Texans that rained down on us yelling and firing like demons, in their appearance more casual and ramshackle than Falstaff's irregulars, whose sergeant could call out, "Howdy, Tom," to his major-general passing by, and the old hero calling back, one man and soldier to another, "Howdy, Bob,"

There isn't much more to tell, tho I will say a word about the prison, but not much about life there for the next months, for there is little to say of that except that I lived through it.

It was a prison called Camp Ford, nearby Tyler, Tex. It was a pleasant enough spot when first we arrived. Some boys from Iowa had been settled there a while. It was an open place, on a hill, with some pretty trees. Those Iowa boys had been able to buy cattle and slaughter it and eat the beef, and there was corn and bread and some of them had started gardens of vegetables and flowers. It was just a big stockade covering some acres on a hill. Life had not been bad for the prisoners there until we came.

"How many of you is there?" one bearded fellow asked as we filed in.

"Don't know," I had to tell him, for I figured we were about the earliest taken back there at that crossroads.

"Thousands," I should have said, for that turned out the truth. By the time I left none of us had shoes, all were clad in rags, there was only corn meal to eat, most of us were sick and racked by the dysentery, we had taken down all the trees and grubbed the stumps and knocked down all the huts for firewood and warmth, and we were all living outdoors in the weather in that stockade. That's about all there is to say about it.

Then one day, when they heard they had lost for certain, the guards went home, and we walked ragged and barefoot out of there, and went home too as best we could.

All that was just behind me, then, when I returned, and so going back to the routine of chopping wood and visiting and the weather and boiling the sap for syrup and going in the spring to town to sell cheese and cherries and fixing a flax wheel and that sled for that lovely girl, all that did not seem dull or tedious at all to me. That was my life, and I was coming back to living it again. All the dullness and stench and killing and suffering of the war was only in my mind and I thought my own real life reclaimed was rich and fine as anything could be.

No, I never married that dear sweet Georgeanne Turner. She moved to Indiana and I never heard she married or she didn't. Later I married an English woman who came to our part of Ohio. But that is another story.

Looking in my diary of that year now I see that I planted corn there by Orwell on May 26 and planted potatoes 5th of June.

As I got on I bought this farm by Mesopotamia here, "between the rivers," in Geauga County, in among the Amish people, and have lived in peace and prospered. I never did go back down South, or anywhere else much, after that, but sometimes sitting here looking out over my peaceful fields I think of that crossroads there and of that blue-eyed Texas devil who gave me back my life.

# THE INHERITANCE

In the afternoon of May 8, 1948 Mark Northway stepped aboard a train in the Cincinnati depot. He was bound for New York City and Greenwich, Connecticut.

The auction to do away with all of General Marcus' and Aunt Ida's possessions was set for May 10 and May 11.

A jovial redcap followed him into his accommodation and deposited his brand new, expensive cowhide twosuiter and his raincoat. It was ever folly to travel East without raincoat or umbrella and Mark Northway could not abide umbrellas. He tipped the redcap a dollar. Usually he was not much of a tipper (his father-in-law, the judge, was the big tipper; he always handed the elevator operator a dime, bending down from his great height in courtly fashion to do so) but today he felt very very good.

He himself carried a briefcase, not the old station-marked briefcase he had carried for years, but a new one that did not zip but locked, his own personal case. He sat and put it on the seat beside him and looked out the window, half expecting to see Louise and the kids waving to him. But they had let him out in front of the station at his direction; of course they were not standing on the platform.

He looked around the small, comfortable compartment. It had a door all his own, which he closed. He had never traveled in a roomette before. He was going up there first class, in style.

Everything about this trip was to be first class. For he was in truth if not in fact the heir going up to claim at least some part of his heritage.

Not that he was going to buy anything. No. He would not spend a dime for anything there that should by rights be his. He was fond of the story of the guy who fell in the mud and came up with a diamond stud. That was exactly what he wished to show them: he had been rooked but did not need it. He did not want to shame them, but to show them.

And more than that he had a deep feeling that he was going up there to see the old boy. Somehow he felt that

Uncle Marcus was actually going to be there, at Willowwood, and they would visit, as they had before. He had a deep and corny feeling in his heart that said: *Okay, Uncle Marcus, I'm coming up there to see to see about this thing. I aint going to sit home like a whipped dog.* He thought the old boy would have approved.

His shoes were new, and his socks were new, held up by tight calf-garters. He wore a new blue suit. It was an elegant set of threads, from Dunlap's, single-breasted with a vest. It felt to him like a set of light chain-mail armor, and if he was anyone today in his mind's eye it was the grand little knight Sir Nigel Loring. He almost wished he had the eye patch, and Louise's scarf pinned to his shoulder. He wore a new blue and white striped four-in-hand; just now he realized these were the Yale school colors, which amused him. He stretched the cuffs of his pin-striped shirt out of his suit sleeves and the deep green stones set in gold of the cufflinks that were a gift from Uncle Marcus caught a glint of light through the train window. Looped across his vest was the gold chain and in his vest pocket the gold watch that had been Uncle Marcus' and which Ida gave him when Uncle Marcus died. It was an elegant watch, from Switzerland. A button flipped the initialed lid open; it kept perfect time. On the chain he had, while rummaging through his drawer this morning, appended, as a touch of irony to his mission, a reminder of who he really was, his old Kappa Beta Phi key from the Kenyon days. That was not what people thought it was, the intellectual's key; KB  was a drinking fraternity into which in those days without much trouble he had earned his way. But, however you read the little key, it was, as he told his oldest son, Bo, all a matter of capacity.

Like life, what happened, how you took it.

In a while the train began to move slowly out of the station. He reached and pulled the blind down. He had no desire today to stare at the Ohio countryside.

He reached in his coat pocket and produced a good 25¢ Dutch Masters *colorado*. It was not like Uncle Marcus' large green Havanas, but it was thick and tightly wound. He lit it, puffed. The smoke was cool and bluish; the ash burned to an intricately ledged and grainy whiteness.

So. He was perfectly calm, content. The demon in him had not taken hold and shaken him since he had decided to go. It was Louise who had been a little bit upset, but she had seemed half-sick this last week anyway. He hoped she was not coming down with the summer flu.

He switched on the small light by his side. From his briefcase he took four documents to look at, or read, and arranged them in order: the Cincinnati morning *Enquirer*, which he had not yet seen; a copy of the Hill school's *Script*, with one of Bo's editorials in it that he'd promised he would read; a copy of Aunt Ida's whole long will that he had finally received; and the gray-paged prospectus of the auction.

This "Marshall Plan" that they had passed in April— my God!—was going to cost us seventeen *billion* dollars to rebuild Europe. Good old Uncle Sugar! He hoped they appreciated it. Well, maybe it would help stop the spread of Communism over there. He doubted it. Americans tended to believe that money was the only answer to everything. It wasn't. What was pretty certain was that war was on the way.

Stassen had beaten Douglas MacArthur and Dewey in Wisconsin. That was okay about MacArthur, you had to be afraid of a military man, they never had been very good presidents; but then Bob Taft had just now come through and beaten Stassen pretty good in Ohio. Bob Taft had certainly gotten his and Louise's votes. This article said that Taft's victory kicked the race wide open. Taft had gotten eleven delegates to Stassen's six. He had now come to hope that if Taft didn't get it, Dewey would. Dewey didn't thrill him, with his little toothbrush mustache, he seemed to lack the *character* we needed, especially now, in the presidency. But he was a steady guy. Stassen seemed like a loser to him. And it was true he wasn't any different than a Democrat, he was for giving all our money to the world. Maybe a miracle would happen for Taft like it had for Willkie. No, the really fine guy didn't have that kind of popular support. He was a kind of philosopher-king type, and Americans never went for them. All that was certain was that anybody could beat Truman. You had to bet on Dewey; he was the money-player in the game.

Boy, the world was in a mess, and on a downhill pull.

Here was a column by Lippman, reprinted from the *New York Times*. It was called "Disorder at the Top."

"It is not, I think," Lippman wrote, "an alarmist exaggeration to say that the Truman Administration is a grave problem for the Nation, not merely for the Democratic Party. The problem is not whether Mr. Truman can be nominated and elected. It is how in the perilous months immediately ahead the affairs of the country are to be conducted by a President who has not only lost the support of his party but is not in control of his own Administration. The heart of the danger lies in the fact that Mr. Truman is not performing, and gives no evidence of his ability to perform, the functions of Commander in Chief."

How true that was! If Bo could just come to write like this, what a service it would be to the nation.

And Mark Northway also agreed with what the guy went on to say:

"This country and the world are in great peril. For we are doing the very thing which all experience warns us we should not do: instead of talking softly and carrying a big stick we are talking loudly while we hesitate and procrastinate about getting a big stick. For though military preparedness is undoubtedly our best insurance against war, military gestures and warlike talk without actual military preparedness is the height of recklessness."

Amen. Well, here was a story about two guys from Pennsylvania who had filed a claim with the Interior Department to the moon! The Secretary told 'em he wasn't sure who owned the moon but was pretty sure the U. S. didn't .

The "hapless Cincinnati Reds" had lost a doubleheader to the Phillies, of all the clowns to lose to, 14-2 and 8-0. It was enough to stretch your faith. . . "a crowd of 20,831, thousands of whom left the park midway in the second game." Fox pitched, the bum. Well, they were playing Augie Galan again instead of Baumholtz and Klu was starting to hit, so maybe they'd do better.

And here he saw that Steve Canyon was still off in some Arab country and had let himself and Lady Nine get ambushed. Yes, sir, a great day for the home team!

So let's see what Bo had said. He began to plow through the piece in the school paper. It was an idealistic editorial on the value and benefits the boys were getting there. "After all," son Mark, or Bo, wrote, "school is by far the most important factor in life—for it is there that the mind is trained, broadened, and prepared for the adventure of life and there that the characteristics and traits which will make or break us are formulated."

It was great that Bo, at seventeen, could think that, and that he was getting such a good education there, and could go on to wherever he wanted for college; but his father hoped and trusted that he himself had not formed in school all the traits and characteristics that would make or break him. He knew damn well he hadn't. He hadn't learned a thing he could remember in East High School, except for the part-time extra work he did, the experience of people and of working for a buck. He had gone off to State as a freshman equipped with a little book Uncle Marcus presented him by Charles W. Eliot, of Harvard, called *The Training for An Effective Life*. In it the old man admonished entering freshmen to a moral life, a hearty quest for knowledge. He warned against the evils of drink and too ready companionship with the opposite sex as deterrents to your cherished goals. That was another age; but if the old guy had been kind of out of it then, in '20, it wasn't such bad advice, even for today. Then they'd decided Mark could better follow that noble course at Yale.

He'd asked Bo if he was going to go to Harvard, after the local Harvard Club contacted the boy. "Knit one, purl two, Ha'va'd, woo woo!" Bo said. That had tickled his father.

He leafed through the long legal-size pages of the will. It was a long list that Ida had left her money to: himself and family, his cousin Harry, his sister Lellie, many others: cousins and kinspeople he hardly knew, had not kept up with. She'd left a pile to charities, a hospital, for a wing to be named for the General, to the nursing home in Cleveland, to Army and Seamen's benefits, to cats and dogs. Actually the total amount, as he now figured it once again, was not what he'd thought it was, or should be. It was surprisingly less. The will really wasn't as bad as he had thought: she'd tipped her hat to just about everyone. The nurse didn't get as much, either, as he'd thought. Oh, she'd gotten a bundle, and nice tidbits to a dozen people in her family. So it went in bits and pieces. But the nurse, Everrest, had gotten the house and all the stuff, the things that were to be sold off, to her profit. Here was the phrase saying that she and the lawyer, as executors, could dispose of it all in any way they wanted, "in the absence of fraud and bad faith." Sure. That was what had made him so mad. The probability of fraud: the crazy pattern of the will, too much to the nurse, the equaling out of amounts to everybody in the family as a coverup . . . That was what Harry, as a lawyer, could have helped him do— break this damn thing on that phrase . . .

He took out the prospectus of all the items to be sold and began to read through it again. There were linens and furniture, porcelain and lace, silver and ivories, rugs, clocks, paintings, glass—Oh dear Gussie, where had it all come from, where did they get all this stuff?

Then he saw that it had come out of storage and from Northway Lodge in Coronado as well as from Willowwood.

His eye skipped here and there:

*Six Aristex hand drawn linen bed sheets; size 90" x 108".*

*Unused.*

*Matched set of eight English, mahogony, Hepplewhite, upholstered seat chairs comprising: 2 arm and 6 side. Late 19th Century.*

*Late 18th Century, English, San Domingo mahogony, pedestal base extension banquet table, with extra leaves and drop legs for full banquet size. Complete with extra leaves.*

*Set of 12 gold encrusted and ivory beautifully designed service plates with hand painted floral centers: signed—S. Stanley. Late 19th Century—Royal Worcester, England.*

*Twelve five crown, 18th Century, Capo di Monte Italian service plates with relief groupings of figures in the border and floral and gold fields centered by different crests of Italian nobility.*

*18th Century 3 piece, French Serve, console set, hand painted scene showing 3 figure group, flower gardens and waterfall. Delicately decorated with and mounted in classic designed ormolu bronze; comprising pair of urns and centerpiece. Date letter—1771.*

*Hand made Italian Rose Point de Venice pillow case. Unused.*

Yes, sir, that was what Louise needed to be sleeping on!

*Carved ivory tankard, Flemish 17th Century, cylindrical tankard finely carved in bold relief of hunt subject: showing animals, birds, forest: surmounted by bear and his prey. Shaped handle, with figures of huntsmen perched above.*

This got ridiculous, in terms of real people, of people and their real needs and lives—ridiculous just like Ida and the General were, at their jumpiest. Like:

*Oriental hand carved tiered Buddhist temple in fine detail. Steps lead to the first cubicle; doors open to reveal an idol. This is roofed and at each of the four corners is hung a small bell. Another room surmounts this. This is repeated for five levels in graduated effect.*

He put the booklet down—it went on and on in close tight print for forty pages—to take off his glasses and rub his eyes. It was incredible, really.

He pushed up the shade, flipped open the General's watch to confirm the dwindling light. It was getting to be evening now. He switched off the light, and stood. He put to rest the cold cigar. Then he opened the door of his compartment and went out into the aisle, heading for the club car. He would have a beer, a good stout Milwaukee brew, to hell today with that Cincinnati stuff.

The train rocked and rattled on, and he sat with his beer, just sipping at it, not thinking of much of anything. His boss Bill Schwarzkopf had said it wasn't really convenient for him to take this particular week off, there were some irons in the fire. Conley wanted them all on hand to see some dignitaries from New York, but Bill guessed they could manage. Mark said he'd take it as part of his vacation, then only take a week or so later. He said he had to go, it was family business. There wasn't, really, if you wanted to know, anything of any importance going on at the station right now. Conley could take his visitors and do he knew what with them.

In a while he passed on in to the dining car. There were some nice-looking people having dinner, businessmen, some couples. The dining car was nice, not as elegant as they used to be, but clean and cheerful and well-lighted. He had expected to find a flower in a vase on his table, but there was no decoration but some gravy spots that made a cryptic design. He sat and studied the menu; then, with the habit of the old traveling man, he took his napkin and methodically and without thinking about it wiped and polished his knife and fork. He had the whole course deal, soup to nuts, with ice cream for dessert. He almost never ordered fish but now he had the trout amandine, not as good as in New Orleans but tasty, with little browned potatoes and two stalks of asparagus not half as good as that he grew in his own garden. Then black coffee, a rarity at night, and yes, by Golly, he would just have a little snifter of the brandy. He felt mellow now again. Looking around at the happy voyagers in the dining car he got a picture of himself and Louise, traveling years ago when Bo was a baby and they'd taken him up to the Waldorf, where they lived then, to see the General and Ida. That was a happy trip, going up. Louise had been excited. They'd had a real fine meal in the dining car while his mother and dad kept the baby. He had known that was to be a special trip, and the old couple had come through generously, with the money and the opportunity in Florida. They had meant it, he knew, to be a turning point in all their lives: for Lellie, his sister, and for him. And he still appreciated it, though it had not been the right thing to do. (And Lellie, they hadn't reformed her either, though they'd kept their hooks in her a while.) That was a trip to remember, even with Ida in the saddle riding high, trying to control them every minute. She was a feisty old gal, all right. But he and Louise kept a warm memory of that trip.

Back in his compartment he undressed, carefully hanging his fine new suit of armor, making sure the door was doublelocked. His bed had been taken down and the coverlet was turned back and the crisp white sheets awaited him. He put on his pajamas and robe and lay back against the pillows. His memory had come alive now, with the thoughts of General Marcus and Ida, and of his relationship to them.

The last thing he had wanted to do was to go to Yale.

He had been happy at Ohio State. He had friends there and he was smoking a pipe and passing a few subjects and in his own mind's eye was a pretty elegant frosh. His main claim to fame that year was tennis. He really had gone at it and had gotten to be good. Was, in fact, Freshman Singles Champion of the school. Tennis was a gentleman's game, wasn't it, and he had expected the General and Aunt Ida to be thrilled and proud over this great honor. But for some reason they seemed to think it was as plebeian as State and never gave him a tumble over it. He had been crushed. It was later, when he went to Yale, and had never been on anything but Uncle Ed's old plow nag out in the country, that they had urged him—hell, completely outfitted him for it, with stick, helmet, breeches, boots—to take up polo. Which he had done, of course. Wasn't bad at it but had been *good* at tennis.

He wished, lying in his bed in the gently rocking train, relaxed but still feeling his years as he recalled the time just on the edge of twenty, on the lip of life as a man, that he had kept up tennis. He had tried to get Bo interested in it but with his bad eye Bo was about as coordinated as a three-legged mule out there. And Luke! After you had pointed out the net and the boundaries to him and tried to explain the necessity for them, and if he could see the net, and after you had tried to convince him that some not total fools in the history of mankind had thought that the sport was not a complete waste of time, it would still be impossible. He had less coordination than old Bo. But Joy had it. Maybe she would come along and be a tennis whiz. Well, he thought, no kid wants to take up what his father was good at. But he himself should have kept it up. He played a tough long-shot game, full of slams. When his wind and speed began to go, he had to change his game too much, the lobbers began to take him. And that was a hell of a thing, when you began to lose to the lobbers! So he'd taken up ping-pong. Right now he had beaten Joy, just this spring, in 122 straight games of ping-pong. He was not just beating her, he was teaching her. He would not let her win without earning it. Right now Joy was beginning to solve his service. Pretty soon she would come along and beat him in a game, if she stuck at it, just like Bo and Luke had.

But tennis wasn't the point. Neither was polo, finally.
The point was the human relationship in it, with Uncle
Marcus, and with Ida, and the family and the sense of
being a Northway, the tradition, and the money. That
pair had pretty much created the family "tradition." There
were two "traditions," Mark thought, that which the old
boy and gal had created, or, really, wanted to create, to
make be so, and impose; then another, very real, quite
historically true, of the early settlers, of the simple folk,
simply a "tradition" of good and unpretentious solid
farmers, with his great-uncle Marcus the first professional
man of note among them. And then his dad too, Tom
Northway, he had been a professional man, much as he
grew not to enjoy his dental chores of peering into
people's mouths. Uncle Marcus had been irate that he,
Mark, would not follow that line and be a "professional"
man also, a doctor or a lawyer. (Harry had done that,
worked very hard to do it.)

But that did not matter, either. The main thing, for
him, had always been the relationship with Uncle Marcus,
the faith and hopes that the old boy had in him, for him.
(He wondered what old Marcus would think of what he
was doing now, managing a television station, most sure
he would not understand it. Uncle Marcus truly was a
man of another age, another time. While Mark had
plunged himself, ironically equipped with his Puritan

work ethic, into this modern time, this electric, consumer age.) All the others in the family had been kind of bamboozled by Ida, but he never had. He went along with her, her domineering nature, and had been about the only one to really love her. And he had, loved her; but, young, he had adored and worshipped Uncle Marcus and what he stood for, his style—had in reality come dangerously close to letting the old boy be what he had wanted to be to him: his real guide and father, the one to take the direction of his life from. But finally he could not do that; he had decided to be a man on his own terms, with Louise leading his own life. And that was what this trip up there, paradoxical as his emotions were, was about: to try to understand what it had all finally meant.

He had studied his namesake as perhaps no one else had, and had an appreciation for him, an admiration and a perspective on him. For the old boy had done a lot, from his being a poor farm boy, worked hard to get his medical education. If he had never married the rich woman and her oil company fortune, he had accomplishments—which no one seemed to realize now—that would have been impressive anyway. Everyone else tended to think of him as a guy who'd married rich. That wasn't fair. Uncle Marcus would still have been something without it. But, by God, it was true he had enjoyed, and used, the dough. It had made him as hard and independent as the diamond stickpin that he wore, let him move with, and be, one of the big men of his time. Be pals with Edison, Ford, Burbank, a friend of Teddy Roosevelt.

Mark had a very old and faded photograph of this great-uncle of his as a boy wearing loose britches and a floppy hat sitting atop a wagon drawn by a nag and piled high with fat sacks of grain on the street of his village. It was a terribly valuable picture to him: it was hard to believe that this boy had become that man.

After high school Uncle Marcus went to Cleveland and graduated from the Homeopathic College in 1872, taking the top prize for scholarship. Later he went to New York State and studied with Knapp, with Roosa and Noyes, and spent more time studying at Bellevue Hospital. Then he studied and observed in clinics in London, Paris and Germany. So he was no slouch of a doctor and he invented a practical Army medical field kit. He was on active duty then during the Spanish-American War, on a direct commission from President McKinley, and went to Puerto Rico on the hospital ship "Relief" where he did research on typhoid fever. And damned if the Government didn't form an investigating commission as a result of his research: it contended that typhoid was spread by flies and not through milk or water. They were pretty skeptical about that then, but the old boy had been right.

He retired from active practice in 1905, when he was fifty-seven and a bachelor. That was the year he met and married the rich widow and learned that oil really could cure just about anything. (Who soon died, and he married Ida, her nurse.)

So maybe it was true: old Emerson's "Compensation" that he had cherished. That always had been his philosophy, or he would have liked it to be. "If the gatherer gathers too much, nature takes out of the man what she puts into his chest; swells the estate, but kills the owner." Maybe so. That was nice to believe, and maybe relevant to Ida's will now. Maybe he should be grateful for his rooking. Oh? So what kind of justice is it that deprives one of his inheritance, not just the dough but the sense of passing along to Northways what was and should be Northways', by chicanery? *That* was the pickle that was too sour for him to swallow.

Emerson said he did not want to find a pot of buried gold, and neither had Mark Northway ever wanted that. He had worked like a Trojan for every penny he'd ever had, after Uncle Marcus and Ida paid for Yale and so tried to put a tyranny on him. Not tried, had: a tyranny that had affected his life, yea his life with Louise, several times in later years, a tyranny mixed also of his love and regard for the old pair. So where was the compensation for that, that tyranny? Should it not come to him now? Or was his "compensation" the life he had, had made himself: Louise and the children, his job on an exciting new frontier. Yes, but still—The pot had never been buried, was always there beckoning in the future, gleaming, glittering—But had been an illusion, a false rainbow, and was now an irony, as he headed to look at the things that should—or he would at least by now concede—might have been his, stacked for auction in the hall of Willowwood. Well, it was buried now.

There was something else the sage had said, an elusive phrase that flew by his mind like an arrow that misses and whose wind you feel as it goes by. Something about fear, the adjustment of equity through fear, that he wasn't sure, only recalling the idea vaguely, whether should apply to him or to Miss Everrest and the lawyer . . . .

He felt too good—or bad?—too high on memory and thought in this long free introspective analyzing yet not quite forgiving moment to want to think about it anymore. . . .

He stretched out as far as he could on the short bed. He had tensed, tightened up, thinking about it all. It was like drinking ice-water after strenuous exercise; he had wanted so badly to stay feeling good, relaxed, to be fresh. He lay like a length of iron on the bed, listening to the clack of steel wheels on the roadbed, trying to remember the Dickinson poem about trains that Louise liked. After a while he began to think of high unmowed grass, of tall yellow corn rustling in his field, of blue rhythmic saltwater waves; and slowly sleep came.

In the morning he dressed again in his new threads and took, for him, a very late breakfast in the diner. The train pulled into Grand Central in the early afternoon. After disembarking he stood a little stupidly with his bags in his hands. It was May 9. The auction began tomorrow. He could catch the New York, New Haven and Hartford on to Greenwich now but he had nothing to do there except to check into his hotel, grab a bite of something. He always felt an excitement about New York. He had always wanted to bring Bo here for a visit, walk him up and down Fifth Avenue. Maybe one day Bo would be coming to see his publisher here. Now it seemed to him that he should take a few hours and do something here in the city. In a moment he thought of Sweeney's and thought that though not really hungry he would take an early dinner there. It was his favorite restaurant in New York. Then he would go on to Greenwich.

He checked his suitcase and briefcase and got a cab and told the guy to take him to Sweeney's. He wasn't your typical New York cabby and offered him not a word of gab, which suited Mark just fine.

He had been to the restaurant a lot of times and thought they had the best steaks in the world. One time he took Lellie's husband there. He was a self-styled gourmet and kind of particular in regard to the way he liked his food. Mark had bet him a sawbuck that he could get his steak cooked exactly as he liked it, which was charred black on the outside and red on the inside. And that was just exactly how he had gotten it. He paid up without a murmur. That had been a good night. They talked a little about old Marcus and Ida, what a rough time they'd given Lellie before she married, and hadn't given them the time of day since. That was just fine with him, Lellie's husband said. How could anyone stand to be around the old curmudgeons? Mark said you had to understand them. Morrie said, eating the steak, he would leave that up to him.

Sweeney's was open, but it was too early for much of anyone to be in there. One old guy was in a corner reading a paper and lapping at a beer. There used to be a lot of ballplayers and other sports types in here. Maybe he was an old baseball jock. No, looking at him Mark thought that the most he ever could have been was an old welter who never learned to duck. He ordered a beer and took it on a stroll around the walls looking at the old photos of baseball greats and famous racehorses that he remembered from the times before. When he sat to order he tried to jolly the waiter by telling him how he'd won money on their steaks and asking could they still cook one charred outside and blood-red inside? The waiter grunted, said if he wanted it rare that was probably how he'd get it, but no guarantee from him. When he did get the steak it was pretty good, it was all right. But it wouldn't have won the bet.

So he paid up, feeling kind of foolish in the now empty place, and rode back to the station and in a while caught a train for Greenwich.

He arrived at the Greenwich station with a crowd of commuters going home and hailed a cab. He had a reservation at what Bill Schwarzkopf said was the best hotel. When he arrived, his room was small but posh. He tipped the eighty-year old "boy" who, wheezing, carried up his bags and sat down on the bed wondering what to do.

Staring at the TV set in the room he decided with great resolution not to turn it on in order to see what they were doing with television in the East. He had a crazy notion to go somewhere and find a bar and have a drink or two.

That was foolish, and the last thing he would usually ever do, and the last thing he should do now.

So like a good boy he undressed and put on his peejays and went to bed.

He awoke stiff as a bone and for no reason that he could give words to, depressed.

The hotel room seemed shiny. He looked out through the heavy green fake-velvet drapes of the windows, expecting to see snow. It was of course an early spring morning. The sun was up, a cool lemon color, and the street glistened with wetness, shiny like the room with its points of silver, glass and polished metallic wood. He shuffled to the dresser—his leg was starting to bother him now from time to time, his left leg, as if he had strained it or had pulled a muscle in the thigh, or had shin splints— and stood looking in the dresser mirror.

A good hot shower was what he needed. (The marks of civilization were ice and hot water as far as he was concerned, granted a stable social order and all possible freedom for the individual.) And a shave. He had a small hint of his dad's jowls but, patting his cheeks, not too much. These days he did not relish the morning picture of himself. He despised the mix of white stiff whiskers in his morning beard. He took his electric shaver and walked firmly into the swank bathroom, doing a few arm and breathing exercises on the way.

Shaved and showered and in his shorts he went back to the dresser and on whim picked up his wallet. All the new stuff he'd bought to come up here: he should have bought a wallet. A new wallet was always a good sign; it changed your luck, financially and otherwise.

Well, Northway, he told himself, putting the wallet down on the dresser, here you are in Greenwich. With a new set of weeds and the General's watch and cufflinks and chain, come up here to proclaim something to them, or to yourself, or to who? Did you think you were going to meet Miss Everrest or the damn lawyer lurking behind a breakfront at the auction? Hell no, she won't be here, you really didn't think she would be, did you? Was probably relaxing out at the lodge in Coronado. She and Simon Slick, they wouldn't show their faces at the auction, knowing that at least some of the family fools might be here. So who were you going to show what? Just exactly what was it you were going to prove—to who? To *whom.*

He looked at the new blue suit he'd worn now for two days straight hanging in the closet and turned to unpack the old brown double-breasted in the suitcase he'd brought in case he spilled something on the other. He put on the brown workaday suit and a pair of comfortable old brown shoes and a yellow and red polka-dot bow tie. He took his raincoat and headed downstairs.

He ate eggs and bacon and drank coffee. It was only eight-thirty and the auction began in the afternoon. It went from three to six, then had another session from seven to ten each of the two days.

He packed his suitcase and locked his briefcase and got in the taxi cab parked at the hotel's door and gave the cabby the address of the mansion, Willowwood, where once he had been a guest and where now all the precious, useless stuff from over the world, collected by the old pair on their many trips, was laid out for sale. He wondered if Lellie and her husband—or Harry and his little broomstick wife—might be there when it opened in the afternoon. They'd think he was crazy, wouldn't they, not noble, to come up here just to behold it all, by his presence to remind them it should by rights be his and they should have fought with him to get it.

They drove through the Bellehaven section of Greenwich. He had the cab stop across the street from Willowwood. As it was before, it was a depressing gray stone fortress of a place. Dear God. He would truly feel like a fool, wouldn't he, wandering around in there among all the elegant junk.

Suddenly he roared out a laugh, laughing at himself, startling the cabby.

"I'm sorry," he said. "Just a real bad joke."

Then he didn't feel like laughing anymore. But he felt good. He felt—*free.*

After a few more minutes looking at the place, he gave a little goodbye wave to Uncle Marcus and Aunt Ida and Willowwood and told the taxi driver to take him to the train station. Louise would be surprised to see him back so soon, but she would understand. He could meet the New York guys, tell Bill Schwarzkopf his "family business" wound up quicker than he'd thought. He would tell Bo and Luke and Joy to stir their stumps and get some work done, they had seven acres and there was mowing and planting to be done, berries to be picked. He would buy a cigar at the stand at the station and put it in his shirt pocket and save it for the trip from Grand Central to Cincy. He was going home.

# THE BRICKLAYER

We children were natural prey to the prejudices and concerns of our father. He held them strongly.

Except for the fact that, after the Second World War, Hiroshima, and the rise of the Bear as Godless Communism, Russia would with dreadful certainty get the Bomb and use it on us, my father's strongest conviction was that F.D.R. had sold out America to socialism, and we were heading inevitably toward a second deep Depression. He had earned this conviction through the turns of his life.

Dad rambled his way through Ohio State and Kenyon without much concern for learning, cherishing college as a place to play tennis. He was pretty good at it, once, the story goes, beating Don Budge. His innate enthusiasm and sense of the glory of American free enterprise led him naturally down the path to advertising. A dashing figure at the age of twenty-five, he married the Homecoming Queen of Miami U. and started his own advertising agency in his native Cleveland. At twenty-seven, in the depth of the Depression, he lost it.

His father also lost what he had. My father sold copper pots and pans from door to door. He began his cursing of Roosevelt, who desperately created the socialistic support network that would surely rob Americans of their initiative and freedom. I was born premature and could not be kept in hospital and barely made it. 'Twas parlous times.

Dad pulled out of it all right, going on to a productive, enthusiastic career in selling and marketing, which somehow transmuted, to his dismay, in my brother and me both becoming teachers. But along the way we had constant lectures on the absolute necessity of learning to do something useful with your hands so that when the other fellow was out of work and destitute, people would still need you, and pay you, to do some basic thing. For, sure as the guy named Franklin D. Shit had gone to court to change his name and when the judge asked him how, said he wanted to change it to Joe Shit, if we were not obliterated first, we would have another Depression and lose in it whatever fancy jobs and titles we had, and our earthly means.

My brother was to be an electrician. I was to learn bricklaying.

These were basic, useful skills and were, my father thought, geared to our respective levels of intelligence.

At any rate, last spring, as I was going to say, I was invited to represent my university at the inauguration of a younger friend of mine as president of a college up in Michigan. I was pleased to do so. I was myself at the time an administrator, a provost, as well as professor and looked forward to joining the other delegates from colleges across the land to the ringing of bells in the historic domed chapel on the hill.

As I emerged from the small airport building looking for a taxi, a fellow hailed me. He was standing, smiling with pride, by a gleaming long Cadillac in high style a decade and a half ago with BOBBY'S TRANSPORT SERVICE painted on the slightly dented door.

Seeing no other vehicle in sight, I allowed Bobby to set me deep within the blue leather backseat and glide me along to my hotel downtown. He had a crossed eye, a few teeth and en route I noticed in the rearview mirror a long scar on his left cheek. Bobby loved to talk, all on the subject of transportation by his fleet composed of this car, a Dodge van, and an old Lincoln Towncar even as we spoke being beaten back into shape to be the premier limo in the stable. He would take me to Detroit for a hundred fifty or to Grand Rapids for just sixty. He seemed rather crestfallen that I was not in need of going either place.

"It's ten dollars to the college. Flat rate. Might cost you more or less in a taxi, but there's no taxis. So what's happening at the college?"

"They are inaugurating the new president there."

"Oh yeah? Bunch of you guys coming in for it?"

"Yes. Probably mostly coming from this and adjoining states. Probably in their own cars."

"Oh." Bobby made a face like what does a guy have to do? "So how do you do that?" he said. "Inaugurate him?"

"Oh, we get on our robes, and they ring the bells and we have a procession."

"Yeah?" His uncocked eye lit up. "So maybe I could drive you in the procession? You see what a shined-up, smooth rider this Caddy is? I could shine her up even more, and all the brass can see her."

"Not that kind of procession. I mean, not a parade. We just march, I think from the library to the chapel, and have the ceremony."

"Oh." Bobby's face went blank.

From the hotel that afternoon I walked along the desultory street, "two miels" as the woman at the desk told me in that Michigander's hard, sharp accent I had

forgotten, to the college. I walked its grounds, beheld its
hills, viewed its domes and spires and visited with my
friend in his booked and wood-burnished office.

Walking back it began to rain. It grew cold and began
to pour. Foolishly I had not worn my Burberry, had on a
tweed jacket getting soggy and the cap with my
university's logo on it that had made my friend laugh at
my own boyish wearing of it, and had a good "miel" and
more to go. I stood at the intersection hoping desperately
not to take pneumonia. The day had been bright, and I
had been happy in it, so foolishly trusting myself to the
weather of an unfamiliar place.

I spied a miraculous something, a yellow taxi, coming
down the street. It slowed, and u-turned and pulled up to
the curb. The window cranked down.

"Use a ride?" the fellow said.

I got in and squeezed some water from my sleeves. It
fell into some sort of sandy grit on the floor. The cab was
disreputable, the seats ripped, the inside all scarred and
dirty. The driver, not looking to see just where he was
going in the rain, turned to say his name was Freeman.
Asked where I was from. When I told him he said, "Well,
howdy! Welcome to Michigan. And congratulations.
You have found the one honest taxicab driver in this
town. Oh, bingo! These shocks are shot. Well, they

should be, this old car has let's see just about two-hunnert fifty thousand miles on it."

He might have been handsome, blue eyes, silver hair, about my age, full set of teeth or a plate, as he kept turning his head around to talk to me, except that his head did not seem to be set quite right on his neck and shoulders. Turning, his head made an odd angle to his body.

"Not many flowers out yet," I said to him. "Of course, there would not be, here, yet."

"No," Freeman said, smiling at the subject. "I was never a flower child, I'll tell you, in fact, I was a hawk, was in the service and all, well, back then, you know Korea. Anyhow, I always was a flower boy! Yes, sir! I dig a great wide plot for flowers in the spring. You ever been to Holland, seen the tulips? Well, you should go and see 'em. I grow flowers even in winter, you see, little tiny ones that they come up through the snow. Called snowdrops. They are pretty, coming up like that in winter."

A pause, then he said, "I didn't drive this old heap 'til four years ago. I was a bricklayer. Broke my back. That's how I come to be doing this. Driving."

"Fell," he said, pulling in the hotel driveway, taking me right to the door. "Yes, sir," he said. "Broke my back. Anyways, where you from?"

I reminded him. The rain was slackening. "My favorite team," he said. "Go Cowboys."

"How about picking me up at nine tomorrow morning?" I said, thinking I did not want to walk however many miles it was carrying my robe in God knew what weather. "And," I said, in a flush of feeling for Freeman, "then I will need a ride to the airport Sunday morning."

Somehow he managed to get his head turned around on his neck and shoulders so he could beam at me as I opened the car door and edged out.

"I'll be here!" he said. I got out before he could manage to offer to shake hands, wet, cold, my shoes gritty from the compound of sand and soil on his passenger floor. "I'll call now and tell that son of a bitch dispatcher I have a pickup for tomorrow morning and the next morning, too. S.O.B. never gives me the good runs. Nine sharp tomorrow. Yes, sir, I will be here."

I came down carrying my gown and hood and cap carefully on a hanger to the immense interest of the young bellman at the hotel door. I asked whether they had a van that could take me to the airport the next morning.

He said they did and I made the arrangement. Outside Freeman was there, standing by his battered hunk of yellow, five minutes early. He smiled and brought his strangely angled body around and opened the door, with a pop and a shriek, for me and tried to take my cap and gown from me. We clunked off; Freeman trying to turn his head on his trunk to talk to me so that a delivery truck almost hit us as we twisted by it into the left lane without looking.

"Yes, sir," Freeman said. "Go Cowboys."

Several minutes later I realized we were going a different route. I looked at my watch. Robing was at 9:15 and we were to march at 9:45.

"Thought I'd go a little different way today," said my friend. "Look there, coming up the street to the right, there? See that? I laid those bricks. Nice little brick house, in with all those wood frames."

"I see," I said.

He turned left and showed me another example of his work. Then we drove by a high redbrick wall and I guessed it, the place where he had fallen and broken his back. A good straight solid wall. "I didn't fall all that far," he confessed, "but I fell wrong. Got a little clumsy in my old age. Surprised the poppyseed out of me, as my granma used to say—"

I nodded sympathetically, as we turned on yet another small street in a direction I sensed was going away from the college. The nonexistent shock absorbers bumped and thumped as we stopped by a small wall, a zigzagged, curving wall intricately made with craft and precision, if you looked at it in detail.

"This here is my masterpiece," Freeman said, pointing at it. But the hand seemed soft and white, not rough and strong as I imagined a bricklayer's hand. It was the hand of a man who planted flowers soon as he could in the spring up here and brought tiny flowers—snowdrops— out of the snow. I adjusted up my robe and rubbed at its hem, which had slid into the grime of the floor of the cab.

As we pulled away I looked at my watch again. It was 9:25.

"Well—it must be a good feeling to be able to go by and see things you did—that you made," I said.

"Yes," he said. "It is. These brick walls, why, they will be here—"

He veered sharply onto another street heading the heap at a strain in another direction. "Don't worry." he said, "we are heading straight for it now. I wanted to show you some of what I built. I didn't do anything at the college, you know—Ha! I guess not, it was all done more'n a hunnert years ago. Nice brick tho'. A kind of darker brick than I ever had to work, I'm trying to think what they call it. . . . It's three dollars, flat fee," he said, stopping his car at the base of the long hill on which sat the domed chapel. "Just the same as yesterday. I sure won't charge you for the tour. And what time do you need me for in the morning?"

I handed him a five. "Keep the change," I said.

"Oh, well—"

"And I guess I won't need you in the morning," I said, elevating my cap and gown and hood and whisking them out of the filthy car. "I'm being taken to the airport."

"Oh," he said. "Well, sir, thank you and thank you for the tip, then."

I nodded to him, peering through the side window, which he had heaved himself over to roll down.

"All right, then. Have a good one. Inauguration? Say, maybe whenever you come back, I'll be working again. Laying brick. Some days I think I might. Anyways, good luck to you."

"Yes. Good luck to you," I said.

He clanked off with a limp wave of his hand, and I turned to walk up the hill crowned by the chapel.